# Olga

*A Needful Bride*

# Danni Roan

Copyright © 2021 Danni Roan

All rights reserved

The characters and events portrayed in this book are fictitious. Any similarity to real persons, living or dead, is coincidental and not intended by the author.

No part of this book may be reproduced, or stored in a retrieval system, or transmitted in any form or by any means, electronic, mechanical, photocopying, recording, or otherwise, without express written permission of the publisher.

ISBN-13: 9798518131149
ISBN-10: B096YZRMBG

Cover design by: EDH Graphics
Library of Congress Control Number: 2018675309
Printed in the United States of America

*"Come unto me, all who are weary and heavy laden, and I will give you rest." Matthew 11:28 KJV*
**KING JAMES BIBLE**

## Contents

Title Page
Copyright
Epigraph
Introduction
Prologue … 1
Chapter 1 … 7
Chapter 2 … 17
Chapter 3 … 38
Chapter 4 … 54
Chapter 5 … 70
Chapter 6 … 81
Chapter 7 … 96
Chapter 8 … 117
Chapter 9 … 133
Chapter 10 … 143
Epilogue … 175

## Introduction

Olga Fortuna loves pretty clothes, sewing, and anything to do with fashion. When her father brings her and her sisters to Needful, Texas to find husbands, she soon discovers that she enjoys making clothing for others more than the idea of wedded bliss.

For years, Olga has managed to have the best fashions on a very tight budget, but now her mind is turning to the needs of a man she barely knows. Working for him is fun and Olga finds the attention of a handsome cowboy fun. Besides, Mr. Harker will be moving on soon leaving her to live a life of her choosing.

Will she be able to keep up the new shop she and the preacher's petite wife have started in the tiny Texas town, or will she give up everything for a man with a rowdy past and too much time on his hands?

DANNI ROAN

# Olga

## A Needful Bride

Danni Roan

# Prologue

Harker Stevenson sat his saddle gazing out over the prairie and the cows grazing below. He'd been in Needful for nearly a year already and had plenty of work when he wanted it.

Along the base of the hill, cowboys rode lazily around the slow-moving herd as they worked the cattle toward fresh spring grass.

Crossing his arms over his saddle horn, Harker watched the sun glint off a stream that ran through the northern part of Texas and his mind drifted back to the dance the night before.

He had never been a man to notice women much. They were all the same, drab, dreary, looking for a husband and home. He was a free spirit who had never signed on full time with any cow outfit. For most of his life, Harker had been a drifter, working when he wanted and then moving on again.

Sitting up straight, he pushed his hat back on his head, thinking of the long years in the saddle that had brought him to the town of Needful. It was a good town. New but growing and folks seemed to want it to be a place where a man could make something of himself.

Harker had never been anything and would never be something in anyone's eyes. A sad smile tugged at his lips, and he chuckled, thinking of the lively Valentine's Day dance not so long ago. He had accompanied the Fortuna girl, Olga, who was making some new shirts for him.

Day work on the ranches had been paying off and it was high time he bought some new duds. Harker hadn't told the young woman what fabric to use, but he hoped she would choose some of those fancy patterns she was fond of. The dress she had worn the night before surely popped with those funny little symbols on them. The woman had called them a Flore de Les. A shirt made like that would be mighty fine.

"Harker, you comin' down to work or you just goin' to lolli-gag all day?" Old Jacks called to him, and he waved, pushing his horse into a walk down the hill.

A lot had happened at the last social, a cake auction to help out the town. At that shindig Cane had got himself well wrapped up by Miss Fanny Fortuna. A rugged stranger had been attacked by Fanny's cat, and Harker had even managed to spike the punch.

The Valentine's Dance was much calmer by comparison but equally fun and his card-playing buddy, Jude Cane had got himself hitched shortly after. Things were changing in Needful, and Harker knew it was almost time to leave.

"Keep your hat on old man," Harker called as he fell in line alongside the herd. "This lot isn't in no hurry."

"Well I am," the old man's face went red and he tugged at his collar. "I'm meetin' Mercy Perkins for supper."

"Ain't you two kinda old to get hitched?" Harker teased. "I mean, what's the point?"

"The point is so we can be together in our sunset years."

"You gonna sit on the front porch of your cabin and rock all day?" Harker's sharp bark of laughter made Jacks scowl. The foreman of Anderson Hamilton's fine ranch was a wise man. He'd ridden herd on the cattle and his younger friend, Anderson as well. An Englishman with a hankering to raise cows had needed an experienced man like Jacks, but now, the foreman was retiring and looking for a quiet life with his boss's mother-in-law.

"Mind your own business," Jacks shot back. He'd been taking a good bit of ribbing about Miss Mercy.

It wasn't that long ago now that he'd ridden off with Cane, another cowboy turned horse breeder thinking he'd lost the woman he loved to another man. "Besides aren't you spendin' a good deal of time with Olga Fortuna? Seems to me you had a nice time at the dance recently?"

Harker huffed, avoiding the man's eyes. "That woman's making me some new shirts is all." He cast his eyes back at the herd. "I figured we could talk business while we were enjoying a social."

"Right," Jacks hid a grin by taking his hat from his head and wiping the brim, even now in late May the sun was hot. "That girl does love to sew. Why she must have more dresses than anyone else in town."

"I wouldn't count on it," Harker replied. "Both Ruth and Amanda have a fair-sized wardrobe, them both coming from well off families back East."

"Well those women have settled in nicely to married life now. Darwin got a good woman in Ruth, an' she don't mind he runs the livery stable." Jacks shook his head. "I wouldn't have thought Amanda would ever learn to live in that cabin out by the springs with Teddy. The girl didn't know how to boil water."

"Nor did Ruth when she married Darwin. His house is even smaller than Teddy's an' now he's lookin' to work with Cane on that horse outfit."

"I'm just sayin' women can surprise you. You watch yourself, or you'll be in for more than you bargained for. Things are changin'. Needful seems to be gettin' gentrified." Jacks added a wink when Harker groaned.

"That what happened to you old man?" Harker's grin brightened.

"Not exactly," Jacks face went red. "There was somethin' about Mercy from the minute I met her. We're kindred spirits so to speak."

"I thought she couldn't even talk when she got here," Harker groused. "On account of a cow kickin' her in the head."

"That's true," Jacks eased his horse closer to Harker. "Mercy got kicked in the head by an old cow years ago an' her two daughters needed to provide for her after their father died." Jacks shifted his shoulders as he put a nicer spin on the events that led the Perkins girls to Needful. "But Mercy could communicate if you listened. She still loves to hum those old hymns, an' see if I can figure what she's thinkin' about."

Harker shook his head. "I'm glad you're happy, Jacks. You've worked hard your whole life an' deserve some joy. Just don't go paintin' me with that weddin' brush. I'm happy the way I am."

"If you say so," Jacks laughed, kicking his horse into a run to turn a calf back into the herd.

Harker watched the old man dart after the cow and shook his head. His own father had been like that, hard working, dedicated to the land and full of hope. Nothing ever seemed to work out the way he planned though, and by the time Harker was thirteen, the farm was gone, his mother had returned to her people, and his father had died of a broken heart.

No. Women were nothing but trouble for the most part. If you didn't have any expectations in life you were never destined to be disappointed. That's how Harker saw the world. There was fun to be had in a good salon, a cold beer, a game of cards and maybe some dancin' now and then. That was plenty for a man like him.

# Chapter 1

"Olga, hurry up, we'll be late for church," Heidi Fortuna scolded as she waited at the door. "Mr. and Mrs. Hampton have already gone, and Papa has checked his watch three times already."

"I'm coming," the fairest Fortuna daughter replied. "I had to make sure my ribbon matched my dress. It's the newest fashion for girls my age." The slightly plump young woman patted the bow in her hair.

Heidi shook her head reaching for her sister's arm. "It's a good thing bustles are smaller these days or I'd never get you out of this room." The dark-haired young woman looked at her sister's fancy dress. Today's selection was a brilliant rust-brown that shimmered in the light. The whole thing was covered in some odd pattern that resembled geometrical squirrels and Heidi's eyes all but hurt looking at it.

"I do rather like the lighter bustle," Olga agreed tripping along without resistance. "I don't have to use as much fabric, and I can make an over-coat or shawl to match. Like this one." Olga shimmied her shoulders making her ample bosom shake, as she adjusted the shiny rust-colored shawl, trimmed in brown fringe, over her shoulders.

"I don't know who you're trying to impress with all of your fancy clothes," Heidi sighed. "This is a cow town, not Paris, France."

"I'm not trying to impress anyone," Olga shot back, lifting her chin as her dark eyes flashed. "I like pretty things, that's enough. You could do more for your appearance too, you know." Olga's eyes raked over Heidi's simple dark skirt and white blouse. Her sister was quite pretty; tall, slim, and elegant if only she would take advantage of it. "You have a lovely figure," Olga added, casting a glance at her own plumper form as she passed a mirror in the hall. "Besides, Mr. Boden might be at church today, and he seems taken with you."

"Nonsense," Heidi said, shaking her head as she turned down the stairs. "The man is grateful that I helped him when Fanny's horrid cat attacked, that's all."

"If you say so." Olga's grin brightened. Heidi was painfully shy and seemed more than content to spend her days working for Olive and Orville Hampton in the Hampton House.

When their father had brought them all to Texas to meet Mrs. Hampton in hopes of finding them husbands, Olga had been resigned to the idea of marrying a cowboy, farmer, or ranch hand. Now, with the dress shop open and orders coming in for new shirts, dresses, and other items, she wasn't sure she would bother with marriage. Being an independent woman appealed to her now that she had a taste of what it could be like.

"There's Papa," Heidi called, hurrying down the last steps and smiling as a thin man with white hair tucked a watch into his pocket.

"You girls are going to be late," the older man said. "Olga, stop fussing with that ribbon in your hair and hurry along. We don't want the preacher to start without us."

"You mean you don't want to miss his piano playing," Olga laughed. The preacher was well known for his musical talents and tended to be rather enthusiastic with the old hymns. No dirge-like tunes filled the spaces of the little church in Needful, Texas.

"Well, it does get the blood flowing and lifts the spirits." Mr. Fortuna grinned.

"Are we staying for the ceremony after the service?" Heidi asked her dark eyes full of concern.

"Of course," Phineas replied. "I want to wish Jacks and Mercy the best."

"But don't you feel badly about him winning

Mercy instead of you?" Heidi took her father's arm, her soft heart hurting for him.

"I'm fine," the old man grinned patting her hand. "I liked Mercy Perkins and I think I could have grown to love her, but her heart already belonged to Jacks." He winked, taking Olga's arm in his other hand. "Good thing he figured out how he felt before it was too late."

"Papa," Olga scolded. "You wouldn't have married Mrs. Perkins if you didn't love her would you?"

"No, no." The old man shook his head. "It was nice to have a body to talk to though. I'm an old man and having someone who knows the same things I do makes for pleasant conversation."

"You have Olive and Orville," Heidi suggested as they traversed the boardwalk leading to the church.

"I do." Phineas nodded. "And if I'm ever to love again the Lord will see to it. I'm more concerned about you girls being settled. Adele and Fanny have both made matches, I don't want you two girls to be lonely when I'm gone."

"Pa!" Olga spluttered. "You aren't that old. You'll be around for years."

"Lord willing, darlin'." Phineas grinned. "Of course we thought we'd have your mama a spell longer as well." The man's dark eyes grew sad but a smile touched his lips. "She was a good woman."

"We all miss her," Heidi said a tear springing to her eye.

"That's why I want you girls to find a love of your own. There's nothing like having someone who loves and cherishes you through thick and thin. I wasn't always the best husband in the world. I was careless and let the things of life creep in, but your mother - God rest her soul, she never wavered and kept me close."

"I don't think I could love anyone who wasn't stayed and true." Heidi looked across her father at Olga as they reached the church steps. "Someone simple with a sweet spirit and contented heart."

"I don't know that I'll ever marry," Olga said, smoothing her dress. "I like making clothes for people and working with Beth Tippert. Independence feels nice."

Phineas Fortuna paused at the top step of the church stoop, his hand on the door knob. "I know Adele wanted you girls to have options, and I'm proud of her for pushing you that way, despite the fact it goes against my wishes. Your oldest sister has a good brain in her head, but even she is seeing that love trumps all else. A good partnership in life, someone to stick with you through the ups and downs makes a difference. Don't forget that."

Heidi and Olga looked into their father's serious face and nodded. At least now, there was no hurry for either of them to wed, and even if something were to happen to their father, both girls could care for and provide for themselves.

"Yes, Pa." The girls replied as the first strains of music echoed through the door.

Phineas leaned over giving each of his two girls a kiss on the cheek. He had succeeded in seeing two of his children settled, and only God knew what would come next. Perhaps Olive Hampton could convince them that one of the men who had signed up for a mail-order bride would suit them.

Olga followed her father into the church, pausing and scanning the crowd at the edge of the threshold. Music filled the sanctuary and her toes felt like tapping to the lively hymn Pastor Brandon Tippert played.

Smoothing the light brown ringlets at the back of her neck and checking her ribbon one more time, the girl followed her father to a bench seat, sliding in next to Adele and her husband Beau.

"You're late," Adele hissed, giving a shake of her head.

"Olga was getting dressed for ages," Heidi replied in a whisper.

"Ssh." Phineas gave his girls a mild scowl.

The singing continued and they all joined in feeling their spirits lift on each chorus.

The shuffle of boots behind them made Olga turn, and she smiled when Mr. Harker tipped his head. Surely he didn't have another order for her yet. She hadn't even finished the two shirts he'd asked for. It was nice working for the man though. He had indicated that he liked some of her favorite fabrics to use as shirts, bold, striking patterns that stood out. Perhaps it would be nice if he asked for another shirt or two.

A hand on her arm made Olga turn to face the front of the church once more, but she could feel Mr. Harker behind her and she remembered dancing with him at the Valentine's Dance not so long ago.

∞∞∞

Harker felt his lips twitch when Miss Olga Fortuna grinned at him. She had turned around, offering him a smile as he slipped into his seat. His hands itched as he remembered twirling her around the dance floor only a month and a half ago and something made him want to do it again.

Miss Olga wasn't one of those willowy girls you saw so much of these days. She had all the right curves in all the right places, and her dark dress with bold geometric patterns on it caught his eye, drawing it to all those curves.

Shifting his weight, the cowboy lifted his eyes to the preacher who moved from the piano to the pulpit as everyone took their seats.

Today wouldn't only be a Sunday meeting; it was also a wedding day for Jacks and Mercy. Anderson Bowlings had given anyone who wanted to attend the service the day off and Harker hadn't hesitated to take it. Seeing Miss Olga was a bonus he hadn't counted on but was pleased to receive.

The message began and Harker found himself torn between studying the girl in front of him and listening to the preacher talk about purpose, hope, and love. Somewhere in the mix, Miss Fortuna turned and offered him a smile making him feel strangely unique.

"As we close in prayer will the elders please prepare for the happy joining of two of our own?" Pastor Tippert called. "It's a day of true love and fulfillment as we see these two wed."

Harker bowed his head as the preacher prayed a benediction on the congregation then waited as

Jacks, dressed in a dark suit and tie, stepped to the front of the church.

A minute later, Primrose and Periwinkle walked down the aisle in pale dresses, holding spring flowers in their hands.

The preacher moved back to the piano - pounding out the wedding march as Anderson Bowlings escorted his mother-in-law haltingly down the aisle and handed her over to the loving care of old Jacks.

Things sure were changing fast in Needful: Jacks getting married and retiring, Anderson working the ranch more himself and the saloon changing from a place of gaming and drinking to a bank and teashop. Harker shook his head. Needful was growing, but was it going the way he wanted it to? Scanning the crowd, his gray eyes fell on his old drinking and gambling friend Cane seated next to Beau. Cane had taken up with Miss Fanny Fortuna rather suddenly that winter and to Harker's disgust had married her recently. Perhaps it was time to get out of Needful before the noose tightened around his own neck.

"Do you promise to love, honor, and obey Jacks for as long as you both shall live?" The preacher's words filled the room and Harker jumped as Mercy Perkin's replied clear and strong with, "I do."

Yes, things were changing fast in Needful and

Harker wasn't sure what his place was in the town.

As the congregation stood to applaud the couple hurrying up the aisle and out the door, Miss Olga smiled and Harker grinned back. It wouldn't hurt to stick around a little while. After all, his new duds weren't even ready yet.

# Chapter 2

The wedding reception, sponsored by Anderson and Prim was really cooking by the time Harker rode up.

Buggies, wagons, and horses filled the far end of the yard, and several wranglers were busy tending the stock as churchgoers, friends, and town folks made their way to the house. Anderson Bowlings had a fine house where Mercy, Prim, and their baby daughter Liza lived.

Food filled the large kitchen and dining room, but Harker made his way through the house, snagging a snack and heading to the back yard where the musicians were warming up.

Old Jacks beamed as he led his new wife onto the wooden floor and slowly started to dance. Something pinched in Harker's heart, but he pushed it away. Women left. Life changed, and a man was best on his own with no strings to tie him down.

The cowboy's toe tapped to the music as other couples began to move onto the floor and a soft hand tugged at his sleeve.

"Mr. Harker," Olga smiled. "I'm nearly finished with your new shirts. Will you be coming to town to try them on?"

"Miss Fortuna," Harker tipped his hat. Everyone in town called him Harker and he saw no reason to correct the woman by adding his sir name. "I'll be in Wednesday if that's not too soon."

"Not at all," the smile returned and Harker felt his skin flush.

Miss Olga was a pretty thing in that smart dress. "I was thinking I might have a couple more shirts done up as well," he said, wondering where the words were coming from. "Do you have any more of that nice fabric with the patterns on it?"

"I have several I think would look nice on you," Olga agreed, her eyes running over the man's broad shoulders and narrow waist. "It won't be any trouble at all."

"Would you like to dance?" The words were out before Harker registered them, but he grinned when the woman nodded. What could a few more dances hurt? He would probably be moving on in a month or two anyway, not enough time for a woman to get her hooks in him.

Harker took the young woman's hand dropping it onto his arm as he headed onto the dance floor.

A few good reels and he'd be ready to sample the feast that had been prepared for the newlyweds. His hand dropped to Olga's side, and he grinned as she turned toward him slipping into the rhythm of the dance smoothly.

"You dance very well," Olga grinned. "I noticed it at the Valentine's Day dance."

"My mother taught me," Harker replied remembering the days when his mother had been with them, and his father had laughed and smiled.

"Is she gone?" The young woman's dark eyes were filled with compassion and angry words fizzled on his tongue. "Yes," he replied simply. "A long time now."

"I'm sorry. It's hard to lose your mother. It's like the moorings of your heart get pulled out from under you."

Harker blinked down at the young woman, his boot catching on a crack in the floor as his attention waned. Shifting his weigh he pulled the girl close and turned them out of the reel before he crashed into someone.

"I'm sorry," he stuttered leading Olga to the refreshment stand. "I was careless."

A warm hand wrapped around his wrist. "I didn't mean to upset you." The young woman's smile was sad and full of concern.

Harker plastered a grin on his face and hurried toward a platter of beef. "You didn't upset me," he lied, "I must be hungry."

Olga grinned as he handed her a plate. "Well I don't think you will be when this shindig is over." Her warm giggle lifted his spirits again.

Harker cast a sideways glance at the girl as she filled her plate, content to follow him along the table. Her words had struck a cord with him, though he had tried to put his mother and her abandonment out of his mind. The ragged wound still had not completely healed after all of these years. Another couple moved to the table and Harker nodded at Beau and Adele. He missed going to the saloon for a drink and some fun with the other hands, but all of that was gone now. Though inconvenient it meant he had to ride further afield for a bit of fun.

Hadn't these young women recently lost their mother as well? How did they carry on so easily with their new lives? Harker shook his head putting the thoughts away. It was different for them. They had said goodbye to a loving mother of many years. She hadn't simply up and disappeared without a word of goodbye or a backward glance.

As he finished filling his plate, Harker found himself trailing Miss Olga to a table where her family was settling. "I'll go join the men," he said as he realized where they were heading.

"No. You're welcome to eat with us." Olga's smile chased away some of the trouble in his soul and Harker followed.

"So you went right over and kissed the bride," Cane said as he swung a leg over a bench. "Didn't Jacks get mad?"

"No," Phineas Fortuna chuckled. "I shook his hand and wished them both well first. Jacks isn't a resentful man. Besides," the old man leaned in. "It's tradition to kiss the bride."

A roar of laugher erupted from the table making Adele, the oldest cringe, but a warm smile from her husband Beau made her soften her scowl.

"Father, you do beat all," Fanny laughed. "I can't believe all that Anderson did for his foreman. Can you believe this?" the new assistant school teacher of Needful lifted her hand and gazed around. "Why you'd think it was family."

"The way Anderson sees it, it is." Cane spoke up. "Isn't that right Harker? Anderson sees Jacks as all but family and of course Mercy is his mother-in-law."

Harker helped Olga to a seat then swung a leg over the bench. "I reckon so," he agreed. "Anderson is a generous man."

"You gonna sign on with him full time then?" Cane spoke again. The cowboy had only been married a short time now, but he already had a horse outfit started, and his wife seemed content to live in a small cabin on the outskirts of the Bowlings' place.

"No, I am not." Harker barked. "I'm a drifter, an' You know it. I don't work for anyone for long."

"You've worked all over Needful now," Cane grinned. "Dan Gaines almost offered you a regular job as well. Now with Jacks leaving you could be foreman right here."

"Too much responsibility," Harker said, stabbing a slice of beef with his fork. "I'll ride for a man, but I'm not ridin' for the brand. It's a fair day's work for a fair wage, an' I'll let you eat my dust when I'm ready."

"I thought you had been in Needful for a while," Olga turned those glimmering eyes on Harker. "You don't plan to stay?"

"No, I don't. I've been here a little over a year already, but I never stay too long anywhere."

"Why's that?" The question from Heidi caught everyone by surprise. The girl was usually quiet during meals.

"I don't know." Harker shrugged. "I like to see new places. Do new things."

"But what about a home and family of your own?" Phineas asked, his eyes skipping to Olga.

"That's not a life I want," Harker said, feeling his neck grow hot. "I stick around a place for a spell then move on."

"And you have no family to go home to?" Olga's voice drew the man and he looked down at her upturned face. There was no judgment in her eyes and her expression was open, concerned.

"No," Harker's voice grew rough as his gaze met hers. "I'm a rambler. That's what I am."

"It sounds lonely." The words were a mere whisper and something in Harker squirmed, like a rattler in a bag. Was he lonely? Didn't he have friends to play cards with and shoot the breeze?

"Mr. Boden," Heidi's sharp call of surprise saved Harker from deeper contemplation, and they all turned to see the hard-looking man saunter toward them on long legs. His clothes were neatly pressed, his suit new, but his worn pistol rode low on his hip drawing the eye.

"Miss Heidi," Boden doffed his hat. "I was wondering if you might like to dance? If you're finished of course."

"Well," Heidi turned looking at her family, but Fanny elbowed her in the ribs making her rise. "Of course."

"That's a tough one," Jude Cane leaned toward Harker, his eyes following Boden and Heidi onto the dance floor.

"I'd say," Harker whispered back. "You think he's trouble?"

"He's no trouble," Olga hissed. "Mr. Boden is just being kind because Heidi helped him when that horrid Midas attacked him at the dance."

Harker grinned watching Cane's face flush red.

"Midas is not horrid!" Fanny protested. "He is a loving and devoted cat."

"Only to you," Phineas said absently as he watched Heidi move into a slow waltz with the lean stranger. "Anyone know who that man really is?"

"No sir," Cane, Beau, and Harker all replied.

"He's probably just passing through, father." Adele looked up from her plate, her statement practical and to the point. "He's been here since about Christmas I believe, staying at the boardinghouse."

"Probably so." Beau patted his wife's hand in agreement. "We get a good many of them as do."

"Drifters you mean?" Olga looked at her brother-in-law. He was a burly man, with thinning slicked-back hair, but the light in his eyes that shone for her sister endeared him to them all.

"Right." Beau agreed, his eyes passing over Harker for a moment.

"You don't look like Mr. Boden," Olga said, turning to Harker. "You are far more pleasant."

Harker sat a little straighter at the compliment, wondering why the woman's words would make him feel happy. "A better dancer too," he added with a laugh.

"It's not the dancing I'm worried about," Mr. Fortuna said. "The man wears that gun like he knows how to use it. I don't like to think of my girl being too friendly with someone like that."

"Mr. Harker, would you dance with me?" Olga stood taking them all by surprise. "Maybe we can get close to Heidi and Mr. Boden and find out what they are talking about."

Harker bit back a burst of laughter, surprised by the young woman's audacity, but he rose taking her hand and leading her back to the dance floor. Not only would it be nice to take a turn with the vivacious and smartly dressed young woman, perhaps they could shed some light on the mystery that was Mr. Boden.

The man had wandered into town, taken a room at the Hampton House and mostly kept to himself.

Everyone in Needful had been surprised and chagrinned when he'd come to the dance and asked Fanny Fortuna to dance only to be attacked by her miscreant of a cat.

"Who do you think he really is?" Olga asked as Harker pulled her close and stepped into the waltz. "Maybe he's an outlaw." The tone of the woman's voice made Harker look at her, but he grinned when he noted the light in her eyes.

"You wouldn't really want that would you?"

"It would be exciting."

"Excitement isn't all it's made out to be," Harker said. "Sometimes people who wish for excitement only find trouble."

"Well, get closer so we can see what he has to say to my sister."

Harker gave the woman a twisted grin and stepped out, pulling her along smoothly as they twirled within listening distance of Heidi and Boden.

It was easy enough keeping pace with the two who seemed to move slowly and carefully around the floor.

"They aren't saying anything," Olga gaped. "They're just dancing."

A chuckle broke from Harker's chest and he realized that every time he was with Olga Fortuna he smiled.

"Sometimes a dance is just a dance."

"That doesn't make any sense," Olga spluttered, giving him a stern look. "We're talking aren't we? Heidi hasn't got a lick of sense if you ask me."

"You look pretty today," Harker changed the subject to something he knew Olga would love to discuss. She smiled up at him, and he grinned again. The woman was easy to please if that was all it took to make her happy.

"I do try," Olga's cheeks glowed with a splash of pink. "It takes forever to get the fashion magazines out here, but I still do, and with what I'm earning making new clothes for men and women in Needful, I can order a few of the designer additions from Paris." She sighed, her eye fluttering as if seeing her lover. "I love fashion."

"You do real good with it too," Harker studied the bold print of the darker geometric pattern on the dress. They stood out, catching the eye, and he liked it. "I know I'll love the shirts you're makin' me."

"You must come over to the shop on Wednesday," Olga said. "I'll have everything ready for a fitting. Can you still do that?"

"That's the beauty of workin' as a freelance cowhand," he grinned. "I get to set my own days off."

"Oh," Olga blinked at him as the music ended and they paused to clap. "You won't need a whole day."

"What if I took you to supper," Harker offered with a twitch of his lips.

Olga's bright laugh caught him by surprise. "The only place to eat in Needful is the Hampton House." Olga giggled again as he led her from the floor. "That's where I live."

"So you don't want me to buy you supper?" Harker felt his brows furrow. He thought young women liked that kind of thing.

"It's not that," Olga patted his arm. "It would be very nice to spend the time with you. It just struck me as funny."

"I guess pickin's are pretty slim around here. Needful is growin', but it's mostly cows and horses."

"There's the sawmill that the Hampton boys run." Olga plopped down on a bench fanning herself. The weather was lovely, but dancing had left her overheated.

"I'll fetch us a drink," Harker smiled. "You stay right here."

Harker felt a spring in his step as he made his way to the refreshment table and a cup of cold punch. He was actually having fun today and this would be a good memory to have when he hit the trail once more.

∞∞∞

Olga twiddled her thumbs, gazing around her at the people dancing, talking, and eating as they celebrated Jacks and Mercy's marriage. She smiled, happy for the older couple and the town itself.

Mr. Harker was right. There wasn't a lot to Needful. The town was growing, primarily due to the Hamptons arriving a couple years earlier. Not only had they traveled to Texas in a wagon train bringing new residents, they had invested time and money into building the Hampton House and the sawmill nearly a year later.

Like most towns, Needful had a general store, now a proper one and not a simple trading post, but still there were no fancy shops or trendy cafes. The dress shop was new as well, and she and Beth were working hard to build a reputation for fine sewing. Most women made their own clothing at home, mending, and patching items as they wore out, but with so much happening in ranching, mining, farming, and the sawmill, perhaps now women would have a few pennies to spend on a bit of frippery. After all most women liked pretty things, didn't they?

Olga's eyes drifted to her sister in her simple outfit. She would have thought Heidi might have dressed up a bit more for the occasion. Mr. Boden was escorting the older Fortuna sister back to the table they had left a short time earlier, but neither seemed inclined to talk.

"Here you are." Harker returned with a glass in hand passing it to her with a wink. The man was rather bold on occasion, but it was all in good fun. Olga wasn't interested in a lasting relationship, and if what he said was true, the man would be gone soon.

"Thank you," Olga replied, offering a smile. Harker seemed like any other cowboy she had met so far in Needful. Several had called looking to Olive Hampton to fix them up with one of the Fortuna girls, but Adele had been right about becoming independent and finding your own path seemed a lot more interesting than marrying on a whim.

"How long have you been in Needful, Mr. Harker?" Olga asked, sipping from her small cup. The punch was sharp and had a funny after taste, but it tingled on her tongue as she drank it.

"About a year," the cowboy leaned against a tree

next to the bench and watched Olga with her cup.

"You must have seen many changes." She tipped her head. "And mail-order brides."

"I reckon so," Harker agreed. He lifted his larger cup and sipped, making a satisfying smack with his lips at the end.

"But you never wanted a bride?" Olga's face heated with the question. "I'm not suggesting anything," she hurried on. "I'm just curious."

Harker brushed a hand through his dark hair, shaking his head. "I have no need for a wife. I live a restless life, an' I don't know of any woman who would want to live on the trail. Besides," the man's gray eyes sparkled, "It seems that even if I had ordered a wife, I might not have gotten one. Every time a new woman shows up they take their own path instead of gettin' matched up by Olive."

Olga giggled, smoothing her dress with one hand. She was feeling flushed after the dance, but the drink was refreshing. She took another sip then turned back to Mr. Harker. "Poor Olive and Peri." The young woman shook her head. "Nothing ever seems to go as they have planned. Of course Peri is busy with her own life now. She and Bear are hoping for a baby just like her sister Prim."

"What about you?" Harker asked. "You came here as a mail-order bride. You have been here nearly six months an' haven't wed."

Olga fidgeted with her skirts. "Honestly, I'm not sure I wish to wed." The words tumbled from her lips and she gaped. Taking another sip of her glass and draining it dry, she shook her head. In for a penny in for a pound she thought as her eyes locked on the lean cowboy. "I like making dresses and shirts for people. If Beth and I can make a go of it I might never marry. Why do I need a man to tend when I can look after myself and not have to wait on him hand and foot?"

Harker's laugh rumbled from his chest. "An independent woman then?"

"Yes," Olga sat up straighter, lifting her glass to the man at her side. "Would you mind? I'm still rather parched."

"My pleasure," Harker tipped his head taking her glass. "Don't go nowhere."

"I'll be right here," Olga smiled, a tiny hiccup sneaking past her lips making her cover her mouth with her hand.

"Here you are," Harker returned a moment later with a full glass of colorful punch. He leaned against the tree again lifting his own larger cup in a toast. "Cheers," he grinned.

Olga grinned, lifted her glass and sipped noting how handsome Mr. Harker was. If she were to ever marry, she wouldn't mind a handsome man like that. Of course, he would have to dress better than this. His faded pants were tucked into scuffed boots and the boring plaid shirt he wore looked like it had seen better days.

"You would be very handsome if you dressed better," Olga observed. "I mean you're a nice looking man." A wave of heat swept over her and she fanned herself. "It is getting warm out here, isn't it?"

Harker shrugged, taking a sip of his punch. "We are gettin' better weather now it's all but summer already."

"What do you want from life, Mr. Harker?" Olga looked up studying his face. "I want to make pretty things and enjoy them. But what do you want?"

"I don't have any real ambition," Harker mused, looking out at the people milling around. "I like seein' new places."

"Don't you ever wish for a home?"

Harker shrugged. Miss Olga was getting rather chatty. "How about a stroll through the grounds?" he suggested. "Mrs. Bowlings has a lovely garden."

"That sounds nice." Olga stood, her head spinning slightly. Harker stepped to her side offering his arm. "It must be the heat," Olga sighed. "I'm feeling a little lightheaded."

"A walk will help," Harker said leading her along a worn path away from the yard and toward a large garden set out in neat rows.

"It is pretty isn't it?" Olga gazed around her, leaning on Mr. Harker's strong arm for support. "When Papa told us we were coming to Texas I imagined a hot, dry, and dusty place, but Needful is full of hills, grass, and trees."

"North Texas isn't like the southern part of the state. It's rather pretty, just like you."

Olga giggled at the words, feeling them tingle all the way down to her toes. "Now don't you go trying to sweet talk me," the girl chided. "My father won't like it."

"I thought your father brought you here to wed. You'd think he'd appreciate a man payin' attention to you."

"Only the right kind of attention," Olga said, giving her head a shake. "Father wants his girls settled before he passes, you see. Losing Mama made him worry about such things."

"But you don't wish to marry."

Olga shrugged. "Perhaps in time, if I find the right person. I suppose every girl wants a little romance in her life."

"You mean, kissin' an' such?" Harker's voice was

a soft purr.

"Mr. Harker, how forward of you." Olga turned as they stepped into the flower garden; a tall trellis covered in honeysuckle was intoxicating as it scented the air. Olga's head spun and she staggered only to be turned into Mr. Harker's strong arms.

"Whoa there little lady," the man grinned. "Don't go faintin' on me now."

"Hmm?" Olga leaned into the man tipping her head to look up at him. She felt light like she might float away and his warm hands on her waist were reassuring.

"I said don't take a tumble." The man's gray eyes twinkled merrily. "I think you were talkin' about romance."

"Uh-huh," Olga agreed, locking her gaze on his eyes. "Romance."

"Like kissin'," Harker whispered his breath close to her cheek. It smelled sweet and sharp and woodsy.

"I've never been kissed," Olga whispered back. "If I never marry, I don't suppose I ever will be."

"You should do something about that," Harker leaned closer, his face mere inches from hers.

"About what?" Olga's brain was fuzzy.

"About kissin'."

"Who would kiss me?"

The man's lips descended on Olga's and her breath froze in her chest as the warm touch stole all thought. She knew she should have protested, but she didn't want to.

A warm, soft, fluttering began in her belly, and she liked the feeling as she leaned into the kiss.

Mr. Harker's hands pressed into her back pulling her closer and she melted toward him closing her eyes as the kiss lingered.

"Olga Fortuna!" a sharp voice cracked like thunder. "What do you think you are doing?"

"Papa?" Olga blinked as Mr. Harker pulled away. She didn't want him to leave. He was warm and tasted like punch.

A hand grasped Olga by the arm spinning her away from the delightful embrace. "Get to your sisters," Mr. Fortuna snapped. "Now!"

Olga jumped, lifting her skirts and hurrying toward the backyard. She had never heard her father so cross before. Her toes tripped as she hurried, making her stagger as she looked for Adele.

"And now for you, young man."

A cold chill ran down Olga's back as she made

the turn around the house. What would her father say to Mr. Harker?

## Chapter 3

Harker looked down at the smaller man who glared at him with squinted eyes and something like guilt squirmed in his middle.

"Mr. Fortuna," the younger man croaked.

"Don't you Mr. Fortuna me!" The white-haired man shook a finger in his face. "What do you think you were doing spiriting my daughter out here? You scoundrel!"

Another man appeared around the corner of the house, and Harker shifted his feet at the flash of a badge on the man's chest.

"I didn't mean no harm," Harker hedged. "Miss Olga…"

"Miss what?" Phineas growled. "You speak respectfully of my girl now!"

Harker swallowed hard as the other man inched closer. "Miss Fortuna was just saying how she'd never been kissed, an' I only wished to oblige."

Mr. Fortuna's face turned red and his eyes bulged. "Scoundrel! Scoundrel!" he cried, shaking his fist at Harker.

"Phineas," a soft voice drawled from behind as the Sheriff of Needful approached. "Is there a problem here?"

"Yes. Yes, there is." Phineas Fortuna spun on Spencer Gaines. "This scoundrel was trying to seduce my daughter. Now, what are you going to do about it?"

"Seduce?" Hark stood up straighter, his gray eyes flashing between Phineas and Sheriff Gaines. Gaines had been the town's lawman since shortly after he arrived, and Harker knew he was fair if a no-nonsense kind of man. "It was just a kiss. I didn't mean any harm by it. It wouldn't have gone any further."

"See. See." Phineas shook a finger at Harker while addressing the sheriff. "He admits it."

"Which daughter was this?" Gaines' asked softly, his blue eyes keen.

"My Olga. Sweet, innocent, Olga." The older man all but groaned as he shook his head. "I want this man arrested."

"Arrested!" Harker's voice squeaked in surprise. "I didn't do anything that warrants arrest. All I did was kiss a pretty girl. Since when is that a crime?"

∞∞∞

Olga almost crashed into Adele as she made the turn around the front of the house. The very person she had been seeking reached out, stopping her in her tracks.

"Olga, where have you been? Father has been looking for you."

"He found me," Olga huffed, her face growing redder when she caught sight of Beau behind Adele. "I'm just going to get some water."

"Adele," Beau leaned into his wife's shoulder. "Your sister is tipsy."

"What? No, I'm not!" Olga's stomach churned at the accusation. "All I had to drink was punch."

Adele turned her head, meeting Beau's eyes. "Are you sure, dear?"

The man chuckled. "I've been a bartender and saloon owner most of my life. I know tipsy, silly, and drunk."

"I'm not drunk," Olga leaned toward them, hands on hips, a slight hiccup popping from her lips.

"Oh my. What in the world have you been

doing?" Adele asked.

"Nothing." Olga felt tears of frustration prick her eyes. "I was dancing with Mr. Harker then we stopped to chat and have some punch. He was showing me the garden." Her face flamed again as she remembered the kiss and she swayed slightly on her slippers.

"Harker, you say?" Beau ran a hand over his slicked-back hair. "That man has a way of making trouble for himself and others. He's the one who spiked the punch at the Valentine's Day party." Beau's blue eyes flicked between the two women. "What exactly were you two doing in the garden?"

Olga opened her mouth to tell him that she hadn't been doing anything in the garden, but the heat in her face gave away the lie. "Nothing," she finally choked out, turning and stumbling a step.

"Bring her along, dear," Adele said, grasping one of her sister's wrists. "We need to find Father."

Raised voices beckoned the trio on and Olga felt trapped with her brother-in-law holding one arm and her sister the other.

The sharp bark of her father's voice made her shiver, and she wondered what would happen next.

"There," Adele said, her skirts rustling as she hurried forward. "There's Father, Mr. Harker, and the Sheriff."

"It isn't Mr.," Beau said. "Harker is his Christian name."

"Oh my!" Olga gasped. "I've been calling him that all along."

"Very familiar," Beau said, his blue eyes dancing as he entered the fray.

"Father, is everything alright?" Adele joined the three men, leaving Beau to hold her sister in place. "Olga's drunk."

"Drunk!" Mr. Fortuna's shout made Olga cringe. "How? When?"

"She isn't drunk," Harker chimed. "She only had a little punch is all."

"She's as tipsy as a monkey in the moonshine," Beau barked.

"Harker," Sheriff Gaines turned back to the man, his voice quiet. "I think you'd better explain exactly what's going on."

"Nothing!" Harker's voice came out high and reedy. "All I did was kiss a girl."

Adele turned, glaring at her sister, then whipped back to Harker, whatever his name was. "And how exactly did she come to have liquor in her punch?"

"That's a good question," Gaines agreed. "Do tell." He crossed his arms over his chest and raised a dark brow.

Olga watched as Mr. Harker or whatever his proper name was tugged at his collar. "I brought her some punch, that's all. How am I to know how it got anything in it?"

"Check his back pocket, Sheriff," Beau called, tugging Olga forward on reluctant feet.

"Now Beau, there's no call for that," Harker grumbled.

"Let me see," Gaines said. "And don't make me add resisting an officer of the law to the list of mounting crimes."

Harker sagged, his eyes flicking to Olga who looked on in horror as he turned his back.

Sheriff Gaines snatched something from the man's back pocket.

"An empty flask," Gaines said, popping the cork and taking a sniff. "Corn liquor."

"No crime in a man havin' a drink." Harker's voice was truculent. "No crime at all."

"Corruption of a minor," Phineas spluttered. "That's what it is. Corruption of a minor."

"She ain't no minor!" Harker growled as Spencer

latched onto his arm.

"I think we'd best take this back to the office."

"Oh please don't." Olga cried, tears burning down her face. "It was only a kiss."

"And what if it had been more?" Phineas hissed. "The man was getting you drunk. I can't believe he had good intentions."

"I wasn't tryin' to get her drunk." Harker sagged and despite his bad behavior, Olga believed him. "I've been spikin' the punch at these gatherings for over a year. No one hardly noticed."

"I noticed," Beau piped.

"You didn't use to come to these things." Harker stared around him, his eyes lighting on Olga. "I didn't mean any harm. You're a pretty girl an' I wanted to steal a kiss. I'll probably be ridin' out of here soon, an' it was a nice memory to keep with me."

"You think I'm pretty?" Olga dropped her hand to her collar.

"Olga!" Phineas all but shouted. "This scoundrel tried to take advantage of you."

"I don't believe that, Papa."

"What do you want me to do?" Spencer asked.

"I swear, I meant no harm." Harker dropped his head. "I'll do whatever you say. Just don't put me in jail. I couldn't stand being locked up."

Phineas Fortuna's eyes glinted as they raked across his daughter. "Then I have another idea," he said, lifting his chin and beckoning Beau to bring Olga forward. "You can marry her," he turned, taking Olga's hand and pulling her up in front of Harker. "You'll have to marry my Olga."

Olga sagged and strong arms caught her as Adele and Beau held her up.

"What do you say?" Phineas crossed his arms, squaring off against the wrangler. "Sheriff, if he doesn't like these terms, I'll file formal charges against him for trying to corrupt my daughter while getting her drunk."

"I'm not drunk Papa," Olga whispered, but no one heard.

Harker's gray eyes skidded around the group, darting like a trapped animal seeking escape. "It isn't right," he protested, his eyes coming to rest on Olga.

"It's your best option," Spencer Gaines said, pushing his hat onto his head of dark hair.

"I'll do it," Harker's defeated voice made Olga's heart shrink. It sounded as if the man had been asked to storm the castle gates or walk into a lion's den.

"Papa don't." Olga felt the tears on her face. The kiss hadn't been worth this.

"Olga, you'll do as I say." Phineas turned, staring her down. "I'm an old man, and I'll not have your reputation ruined. Do you understand?"

"Yes," Olga dropped her eyes to her shoes.

"Now then." Phineas turned back to Harker. "You two are officially engaged. You work out a story between you. You are not to be alone without a chaperone from here on out. Do you understand?"

"Yes sir." Both parties agreed as one.

Olga looked up, meeting Harker's haunted eyes.

"Adele, if you'll stay here and keep an eye on these two, I'll fetch Heidi, and we'll go home." He cast a scathing look at Harker then turned away.

"Looks like you got off easy," Spencer Gaines leaned in to speak to Harker, but Olga heard. "Olga's a fine young woman."

Harker watched as the Sheriff sauntered away,

and Beau pulled his wife to the side. He was now alone with Olga, something he had wanted very much a short time ago.

"I'm sorry," he said, dropping his eyes to the ground. "It was just a bit of fun." Gray eyes rose to meet brown, and he sighed. "I'd never have hurt you or taken advantage, I swear."

"I don't know why," Olga spoke, "but I believe you. I can't say it was a very nice trick though. I thought we were becoming friends. I." she licked dry lips. "I already told you I don't wish to marry. I want to work in my dress shop and see what I can do. Now look at this mess. Father will set a date and expect us to be there."

"I don't know what else to say. I know I'm a coward, but I can't go to jail. It would kill me."

"It won't come to that," Olga pulled her small cape tighter around her shoulders. "We can carry on as an engaged couple for a bit, then I'll turn you loose. I'm sure father will see reason, sooner or later."

"You don't mind?"

"No, I'll be the Needful bride who jilted her fella."

A wan smile flitted across the girl's face and Harker relaxed. "Thank you."

"We'd better get our story straight, though." Olga looked behind her where her father was approaching in the wagon. "We've met a few times," she grinned. "We'll tell everyone that you knew almost from the beginning that I was the one for you. You'll be devastated and heartbroken when I break up with you."

"That's rather harsh, isn't it?" Harker tried, watching as the wagon approached.

"Well, I am the wronged woman in this case," Olga lifted her chin, smoothing her dress. "I should get to be the one to break someone's heart."

Harker shook his head but then nodded. "Alright. I'll do my best to seem the lovesick puppy."

"I still expect that supper," Olga grinned, though the light didn't reach her eyes. "Wednesday?"

"Wednesday," Harker agreed then turned toward the bunkhouse at the far end of the ranch. "I'll see you then."

Olga turned, her toe catching in the grass and she stumbled, but a firm hand on her elbow steadied her.

"I guess I'd better get you to your wagon," Harker said, his hand warm on her arm.

"You probably should," Olga agreed. "My head is feeling funny." She looked up in time to see

Harker's face flush.

"I didn't put much in the punch," he whispered.

"I've never had alcohol before," the girl replied.

"Never?"

Olga shook her head. "We weren't raised that way even if Adele did marry the town saloon owner. She did it for us." Olga stopped meeting his eyes. "She wanted us to have options and if she married well, we wouldn't have to hurry to the altar."

Harker swallowed hard, guiding Olga the rest of the way to the wagon and helping her up. He hadn't realized the sacrifices made on behalf of the Fortuna girls.

As the wagon lurched forward, Olga turned, looking back at the man. He was still handsome, but now she wasn't sure what she thought of him.

∞∞∞

Harker stumbled his way to the bunkhouse, his head spinning with his present predicament. How was he supposed to live up to his part of this deal? He'd been a fool to think no one would notice the punch was spiked. It wasn't like it hadn't happened before, but it was all in fun.

Walking into the empty building, he slumped to his bunk, collapsing on his bed. He could saddle a horse and ride out. Hit the trail and never look back.

The thought, though tempting, wrankled, and he sighed realizing he couldn't do it. He had already seen the sorrow and disappointment in Olga's eyes. He hadn't meant to hurt her. She was a pretty girl with a mind of her own. One kiss, one simple, stupid kiss shouldn't have caused all this fuss.

Running his hands through his hair, Harker remembered the feel of the young woman in his arms. She had leaned into that kiss, making it thrilling. "A good memory," he whispered. "That's all it was goin' to be, a nice memory to carry with me when I traveled the lonely trails."

Shaking his head, Harker thought through his time in Needful. He'd had plenty of work, made decent pay, and never worried where his next meal was coming from. When Beau was still running the saloon properly, Harker could count on a few drinks and a game of cards. He'd even ridden into town on a Saturday night to hear the preacher play the piano for the barkeep.

Harker shook his head again. Maybe Needful, Texas made people crazy. The stringbean of a preacher had made a bargain with Beau to play the piano on a Saturday night if he could use it for church on Sunday. "Now, look where he is," Harker growled. "Married. Beau, married. Cane, married. Why this whole town is wedding crazy."

The door opened and Jacks walked in, a smile on his face.

"What are you doin' here?" Harker asked, sitting up and plopping his boots on the floor. "Aren't you an' Miss Mercy goin' away on your honeymoon?"

"We are," Jacks grinned. "I stashed something in here though as a surprise. So what are you doin' here?"

Harker didn't know why he did it but he poured out the whole story in a steady stream.

"So now I'm engaged to Olga Fortuna, whether I want to be or not."

The sharp bark of laughter from the old foreman was not what Harker had expected, and he glared at the older man.

"You think that's funny?"

"The good book says, 'Be sure your sins will find you out.'" Jacks grinned. "Now you have to pay for those sins. Maybe this is a time where you can reflect on your purpose in life, Harker. Just because you've always been a saddle bum doesn't mean you have to stay that way."

"Keep your advice to yourself old man," Harker grumbled. "As soon as that chit turns me loose, I'll hit the trail for good."

"Good luck with that," Jacks said. "Maybe I'll see you around town when I get back."

Without another word the older man picked up a box of women's boots and hurried outside, leaving Harker to his misery once more.

Flopping back onto the bed, the cowboy gazed at the bunk above. How did a man go about pretending to be engaged to a girl? Was he supposed to make a fuss? Did he bring her flowers?

Flopping over onto his stomach, the lean man buried his head in his pillow. He wasn't about to make a fool of himself over a woman. His father had pined away, waiting for his mother to come back. But no, Harker Stevenson wouldn't play the fool. He'd serve out his time, and as soon as Olga was done with him, be on his way.

The girl had already told him she wouldn't wed. What harm could calling on her to her father's wishes bring?

A grin tugged at his lips as he thought on the problem. If he was engaged to the girl, didn't that mean he could kiss her again?

Turning over, Harker placed his hands behind his head and started to whistle. Perhaps two could play at this game Mr. Fortuna had set in motion. If he could convince the old man he wasn't the right match for his girl, maybe this whole charade would come to an abrupt end.

"And that kiss was sweet," Harker whispered, chuckling in the darkening room. A week or two and he was sure both Phineas and Olga would be happily rid of him.

The trail beckoned, and he began to figure on what he would need and where he would go next. He'd heard tell of a strange place out west where the water boiled and the sky hissed. Maybe he'd head out that way and see if it was only tales from the muddled minds of mountain men.

Yes, a few more weeks and Harker Stevenson would be free as the wind. No fences, not hobbles, and no woman to hold him in. That old itch tingled at the edge of his spine and he knew that it was time to leave Needful. He was done with Texas, but he would be leaving better off than he had arrived.

"She doesn't want me anyway," Harker said again. "It won't be long now, an' I'll be on my way."

Standing, Harker rummaged through the box at the end of his bunk, counting out the money he had saved. He would have ready cash, his string of good horses, and a few fancy new duds. What more could he ever need?

## Chapter 4

The following two days, Harker worked harder than he had in ages. With Jacks gone away, Anderson seemed to feel he needed every hand on deck.

"You mind running that branding outfit down on the back quarter?" the boss man asked, his clipped English tones sounding funny in Harker's ears. "Jacks says you're a top hand and can manage if I let you."

"I can do it," Harker agreed. "Looks like I'll be sticking around for a bit longer anyway."

"Yes, I heard you're courting the lovely Olga Fortuna." Anderson's eyes sparkled as he thought of his own Needful bride.

"Uh-Huh," Harker replied, tipping his hat and pushing his horse toward the back forty. He had no desire to talk to Anderson Bowlings about his new situation. It already chafed that he couldn't leave town without looking over his shoulder for the law. Mr. Fortuna seemed an easy-going sort, but on this one point, the cowboy was sure Phineas would file charges if Harker left town.

By Wednesday, tired sun-blasted and weary, Harker made his way back to the bunkhouse, washed up and headed for town.

The sun was setting low on the western horizon when he pulled his horse to a stop in front of the Hampton House and swung down.

"You're here?" Olga's voice caught him by surprise as she came around the corner of the house. "I'm just leaving the shop." Her smile was bright and she held a neatly wrapped package in her hands. "I brought your shirts. Would you care to try them on?"

Harker nodded, his brain slowly catching up with his eyes. The young woman looked smart in a contrasting striped dress, the design tapering to her waist and making her look less plump than she was. "Whatever you say," the words popped out as a grin spread across his face. The girl did dress pretty.

"Olga, there you are." Heidi stepped out of the boardinghouse. An apron snugged around her slim waist. "Papa is looking for you." The dark-haired girl blinked, studying her sister. "Is that what you wore to work today?"

"Yes," Olga smoothed the delicate fabric.

"Where did you ever get those colors?"

"I got them back home," Olga grinned. "I've been working on this dress for a bit in between orders. I think it came out rather nice."

"It looks fine," Harker agreed, slipping up to Olga's side and to offer her his arm. "I believe you were goin' to fit me for those shirts."

"But the colors," Heidi blinked, "Maroon and gold, like some kind of mixed up bumblebee."

Olga caught her sister's quiet words as she led Mr. Harker back toward the shop. Beth was just closing up and could serve as a chaperone, complying with her father's wishes. Perhaps Heidi didn't like the bold colors of the dress, but the fabric was of the highest quality, and Olga had been able to get it for a price that would make your head spin.

"We'll just nip over to the shop," Olga said, smiling at Mr. Harker as if she was happy to see him. "Beth will still be there," she added loudly for her sister's sake.

"I'm lookin' forward to seein' what you have for me," Harker replied. He was tired, but the young woman's bright smile and cheerful outfit lifted his spirits.

"Did you have a good week so far?" Olga asked, her hand on his arm.

"It's been busy." Harker shook his head. "With Jacks retirin' an' startin' his new life, Anderson is working us all harder than ever. I think he's afraid it will all fall apart without old Jacks."

"Do you think it will?" The young woman's voice was filled with concern.

"No," Harker chuckled. "Jacks hired good men an' sooner or later, Anderson will make someone the new foreman. I think Michaels is in the running an' maybe a few more."

"Do you plan on staying?"

"No, I'll hit the road once," he paused, waving his hand in a broad circle, "once this is all over."

To Harker's surprise, the young woman giggled. "Well, it is a different kind of trail, isn't it?"

Harker smiled, tipping his hat back on his head with his free hand. "I reckon it is. It will make a funny tale if nothin' else."

"Don't worry, Mr. Harker." Olga stopped suddenly pulling him with her. "I'm sorry, I assumed your name was Mr. Harker, but Beau says that is your Christian name. So it isn't appropriate to call you so."

Harker chuckled, feeling lighter than he had since Sunday. "It's Stevenson, Miss Fortuna. Harker Stevenson."

"Well then, Mr. Stevenson, shall we continue."

A few minutes later, Harker found himself inside the downstairs of a small shop that Miss Olga and Mrs. Tippert shared with Mr. Franco, who gave music lessons to the town's children. The space was small but neat and Harker's gray eyes flitted over stacks of fabric and two tables covered with pincushions, needles, and thread.

"The changing room is right there," Miss Olga said, pointing to a corner covered in curtains. "Don't worry. We won't peek." She added, garnering a laugh from Beth.

"I thought you'd gone home already?" Beth Tippert said, pushing a lock of golden hair back into its loose bun.

"I met Mr. Stevenson on the way and brought him back to try on his new shirts."

"It's nice that you're making him new shirts, what with your engagement and all."

Olga squirmed, listening to the man stripping out of his shirt. "Well, yes. He had ordered them earlier, of course."

"I know, but now things have changed. I know

your father has been in to talk to Brandon about a wedding."

Olga felt the blood drain from her face. "He did?"

"Yes. Brandon told me at lunchtime today."

"Oh." Olga's heart skipped a beat. She didn't want to marry. But, she was sure that she and Mr. Harker, no Mr. Stevenson, would be able to avoid her father's plans. "I'm sure he'll mention something tonight."

"This one is rather tight in the shoulders," Harker stepped out of the curtained room, tucking the last bit of shirt into his pants.

"It looks very nice," Beth said, her voice passive.

"I like the pattern," Harker looked up and smiled, seeing something in Olga's eyes that turned his stomach.

"Yes, it's very nice on you," Olga smiled, the flicker of worry skidding away. "Turn around so I can see."

The woman fussed over his shirt, adjusting things, her warm hands brushing his shoulders and waist, almost tickling. A moment later, he was back in the curtained area putting on the second shirt. This one he liked even better with the tiny wheat-like pattern dotting it all over.

"This one's perfect." Harker couldn't hide his grin. He couldn't remember ever owning a shirt that fit so well or popped with such brightness.

"It looks lovely," Olga agreed. "Yes, I'll just let the other one out a smidge. I'll have it for you by Friday."

"Olga is a wonderful seamstress," Beth agreed, her eyes flickering over the bright yellow shirt. "I'm sure you'll cut a bold swath with that shirt."

Harker grinned. He felt oddly special with all of the attention. He had been on his own a long time, riding dusty trails, working cow camps, silver mines, and big farms, nothing more than a cog in the gears of someone else's life. Now, with Olga looking at him with that bright smile, he felt like he was someone.

"Shall we go to dinner?" he asked. "I think I'll wear this now if that's alright."

"I think it's a wonderful idea," Olga agreed. "Our colors compliment."

A bright smile stretched across Harker's face and he hurried to gather his other shirt. Tomorrow he would be back to the dust of cattle work, but tonight, he could make a memory with a pretty girl.

"Good night Beth," Olga called as the cowboy held the door for her. "I'll see you tomorrow."

"Good night," Beth replied, shaking her head as the two walked into the street.

"I'm afraid I have something to talk to you about," Olga whispered as Harker offered his arm. "Beth just told me that Papa was talking to Pastor Brandon about a wedding."

"Already?" Harker tugged at his collar that suddenly felt tight.

"I'm afraid he's going to try to hurry us into something." Olga shook her head. "Father is usually a very easy-going sort, but he's got a bee in his bonnet on this one. He's determined to see his girls married and, well, I don't know what he's thinking."

"What if he forces our hand?" Harker asked, licking his lips. He had been having a pleasant time with the young woman until this news had settled around his neck like a noose.

Olga stopped, turning and placing a hand on his chest. "We need a plan," Her dark eyes searched his. "I don't want to see you go to jail for nothing more than a kiss." Her cheeks flushed and Harker licked his lips again, this time remembering the kiss. "I also can't hurt Papa by defying him."

"You'd make me marry you?" Harker whispered.

Olga tapped her lips with a finger. "Maybe."

"What?"

"Ssh!" Olga tapped his chest with that same finger. "I have an idea."

Harker tugged at his collar, choking. "I hope it's a good one. You said yourself you didn't want to be married."

"What if?" Olga stopped looking up and down the street. "What if we went through with the wedding then left and got an annulment. No one could stop us."

Harker lifted his hat, wiping his brow with the bandana from his back pocket. "I don't know. It sounds tricky."

"You said yourself you'd like to hit the trail. We could go to Houston or Dallas and find a magistrate that would declare us 'unwed'."

"Maybe it won't come to that," Harker hedged.

"Olga!" Phineas's voice echoed down the boardwalk. "Come in off the street." The older man's dark eyes flashed as he watched her with Harker.

"Come on," Olga said, taking the man's arm. "It will be just like make-believe."

Harker placed his hat back on his head and let the girl lead him toward her father. How had he gotten himself into this mess? Sweat beaded his forehead again, but he ignored it. His freedom was at stake here.

"Papa, Mr. Stevenson was just trying on his new shirts. Doesn't he look smart?"

"If you say so," Mr. Fortuna scowled. "I told you, you weren't to be alone with this scallywag."

"We weren't alone," Olga sighed. "Beth was there." She pointed toward the shop where the preacher's petite wife had just closed the door.

"Humph," the old man said. "Come in. Dinner is waiting."

"I'm eating with Mr. Stevenson." Olga grinned. "Or should I call him Harker now that we're engaged?"

Harker watched the old man's eyes harden, but he didn't say anything.

"Suit yourself," Phineas barked. "But if you step out tonight, you take Heidi with you."

"Yes sir." Olga flashed Harker a grin as if this whole situation was a lark. Didn't she understand what was on the line?

A few minutes later, Harker found himself seated at a cozy corner in the back of the Hampton House dining area. One of the Hampton daughters-in-law stopped by bringing coffee and water then returned with a tray of food.

"It's nice to see you with your new beau," Shililaiha grinned. "Enjoy your dinner."

Olga offered the other woman a wink then leaned across the table from Harker. It was time to make everyone believe he was the one for her.

Harker looked into Olga's eyes, seeing a mischievous light and his stomach bubbled with nerves.

"This is where you make everyone believe you're madly in love with me," she chuckled.

∞∞∞

Olga let the giggle building inside her bust and watched as Harker's eyes grew wide. The man was far too worried over this whole thing.

"Enjoy," Shililaiha grinned, placing plates before them. "I hope you had a good day at work," she added, returning Olga's wink.

"I did. Don't you think Harker looks nice?" Olga waited, watching to see if Shi would react to her using the man's first name.

"It looks brilliant," the young woman agreed, her brows rising. "Quite bold."

Olga watched Harker grin as some of the tension from his confrontation with her father bled off. "He seems to lean towards bold."

"You don't find much that stands out these days," Harker replied. "Everything looks the same."

Olga felt the flutter of joy with the compliment. Her sisters never appreciated her ability to make high fashion on a shoestring budget. They always chose the simplest fabric. Olga had a knack for finding bargain basement items that others didn't seem to want. Silks, satins, and other materials that were perhaps a bit bright but the highest quality.

"The shirt should wear well also," she finally spoke as Shi sashayed away. "I only use the best quality materials."

"You put pride in your work," Harker replied, lifting his fork. "That's a good thing."

Olga nodded. "I love pretty things." She lifted one shoulder in a shrug. "I always have. My mother taught me to sew when I was nine, and I made my first dress from a flour sack. I haven't stopped since."

"You enjoy it?" Harker dug into his bowl of stew.

"I do." Olga reached for a fresh slice of bread, buttering it and handing it across the table absently then started on another one. "Don't you?"

Harker stopped his fork halfway to his mouth. "I work hard."

"But do you feel a sense of pride in what you do?" Olga bit into the freshly buttered bread.

"I never thought of it," Harker admitted. "I do my best for whoever I ride for. Anderson seems pleased with my work this week. He put me in charge of some brandin' on the back forty."

"That's good." Olga studied him as she chewed another bite of bread. "But how do you feel about it all?"

Harker dug into his stew, eating several bites before answering. "I've been riding so many places," he began, "I don't reckon it matters much to me. I do the work that keeps me fed an' clothed an' able to go where I please."

"It sounds like an adventure." Olga grinned, but her eyes were troubled. "Don't you ever want to settle down?"

"No." Harker's reply was quick. "My pa worked himself into an early grave an' never amounted to anything. I don't see the point in slaving away when I can keep food in my belly an' meet my needs workin' for someone else."

"Do you have any other family?" Olga's brown eyes were soft, something flickering in their depths.

"Nope."

"That must be lonely?"

"Don't see why?" Harker said. "I've been a free spirit for a long time."

"And that's enough?"

"Seems to be," Harker grinned. "I can come an' go as I please. I can work or not work depending on my mood an' there's always somewhere else to see."

"What about if you can't find work?" Olga's curiosity was getting the better of her. "What do you do then?"

"I ride on."

Olga sighed. She didn't know if she could ever live that kind of life. She had her family and now the dress shop. She loved what she was doing and the sense of independence was liberating. She never needed to be a burden to her father again.

"I feel that way with my dress shop. At least, I think I understand. Father has been worrying that his girls won't have anyone to care for them when he's gone. When Mama died, it threw him for a loop. That's why we came to Needful. He thought he could find husbands for us, and we'd be looked after." A smile tugged at her pretty lips. "Now, I have a way to support myself and he shouldn't be worried."

"He still seems determined to have you wed," Harker growled. "Whether you want it or not."

"He's just worried," Olga replied. "We'll turn him around." She giggled. "Or," she placed her finger along her nose, "We'll take matters into our own hands."

"Olga, Mr. Stevenson," Phineas walked up to them. "I hope you're enjoying your dinner."

"We are," Olga grinned. "Harker was telling me about his life and his travels."

The older man's brows rose at the use of Harker's name in such a casual way.

"Sounds like he's been a saddle tramp from what I've heard. I hope you aren't thinking of ducking out of town," he added, giving the man a hard look.

"No, sir. I might not be a man who stays in one place long, but that doesn't mean I don't live up to my word."

"Good. I'd hate to put the law on you."

Olga watched as a shiver raced down Harker's spine, and her heart went out to him.

"Now, Papa, don't be that way. We're having a nice dinner and getting to know each other."

"I made an appointment with the preacher," Phineas said, cutting his daughter off. "We'll be having a wedding in two weeks. I'm not having anyone take advantage of my girl then ride away."

"But," Harker spluttered. "That ain't right!"

"You know the alternative." Mr. Fortuna turned, walking away without a backward glance or an opportunity to argue.

"Oh my," Olga gasped. "This is getting interesting."

"Interesting?" Harker choked. "You're father is goin' to make you marry a man you don't want."

"Well, we'll see." Olga grinned. "I guess I should start making a dress, just in case though."

"You'll go through with it, won't you?" Harker's voice was flat.

"Yes. I think I will." Olga's bright eyes danced. "We'll get it annulled in a few weeks. Don't worry."

## Chapter 5

Two weeks later, the wedding took place with the sheriff as best man, and a glinty-eyed Phineas giving the bride away.

Harker felt the itch between his shoulder blades like a shotgun or bowie knife was tickling his spine. He scratched at the back of his neck as the preacher smiled down at him, making him squirm more.

Olga had continued to assure him it wouldn't come to this, but here he stood in a new suit, his boots polished, and his hair slicked down to his head. How an innocent, well, mostly innocent, kiss had led to this he didn't know, but here he was, his back to the wall being forced to marry despite his wishes.

The door of the church opened, and he lifted his gray eyes from examining the tips of his worn boots and saw Olga step through the door on her father's arm. The young woman smiled, giving him a tiny wave as she floated toward him in a pale dress piped with dark ribbon around the low bodice, dropped waist, and hem. Harker smiled slightly, despite the pounding of his heart. His eyes flickered between the preacher, sheriff, and the pair marching steadily toward him. As foolish as this whole debacle seemed, Harker knew one thing. He could easily leave a wife behind, but a stint in prison, even a short one, would break his spirit like his mother had broken his father's.

"Hi," Olga grinned at him as her father stopped in front of the preacher.

"Hi," Harker croaked, his voice rasping painfully in his throat.

"Ssh," Phineas ground.

The preacher began to speak, and Harker turned toward him, each word asked for given in a hoarse whisper.

The older man returned to a seat next to his other daughters and Harker shuffled closer to the girl holding his hand. "Can you keep your promise?" he asked as the preacher turned to take a ring from Sheriff Gaines' hand.

"I won't back down," Olga assured him, her dark eyes bright, as air returned to Harker's tight chest. "What do you think of my dress?" she hurried to ask.

"Pretty," Harker smiled as his head spun a little.

"You need to put the ring on her finger," Brandon Tippert said, nudging Harker.

A moment later, the preacher pronounced them wed and Harker felt Olga squeeze his hand as a smile broke across her face.

"You may now kiss your bride," Tippert said.

Harker leaned in, prepared to brush his lips across Olga's, a gentle, chaste kiss that would show he had honor. But instead, as his mouth met hers, her arms flew around his neck and she pulled him close, kissing him boldly as sparks danced in his head.

A roar of laughter rippled through the church, and Harker gently pried Olga's hands from his neck.

"Please welcome Mr. and Mrs. Harker Stevenson to our midst," the preacher chortled. "I think they were made for each other."

Harker turned, giving the preacher a hard glare and handing him a few dollars for his service before tugging Olga back up the aisle in ground gobbling strides.

"That was fun," Olga laughed, practically racing to keep up. "Did you see my sisters' faces when I kissed you?" A warm laugh bubbled from her and Harker shook his head.

"What will your father think?" he asked, his head still fuzzy as if he'd had one too many beers at the old saloon.

"He'll think we surrendered," Olga said, her eyes flashing with delight as her spine stiffened. "Now come on, they're having a party, and we don't want to miss that."

"Are you ready to leave tonight?" Harker asked as they walked toward the Hampton House and the wedding supper.

"All packed," Olga giggled, "just like we agreed." She tipped her head as he slowed his pace. "Do you think we should wait? It might give Father some time to think it through."

"If we wait, we might not get an annulment," Harker said. "We leave tonight headed for Houston."

"Alright," Olga agreed. "I do hate to leave the shop and Beth on her own though."

"You'll be back in less than two weeks," Harker said. "Free as a bird an' ready to run your shop unhindered."

"That's true."

Together they stepped up onto the small stoop at the front of Needful's only boardinghouse. They had hurried away so quickly they hadn't even had time to shake hands with their friends.

"Congratulations!" A familiar voice chimed as they walked into the dining room. "I never thought I'd see the day you got hitched."

"Jacks," Harker growled. "I see you made it home in time for the proceedings."

"Mercy was missing her girls and that grand-baby," Jacks grinned as his wife walked toward them, a smile on her face. She was humming and Olga strained to hear the tune.

"That's *Let the Lower Lights be Burning*," Olga said. "I love that song."

Mercy smiled that crooked grin, with a sweet light in her eyes. "Con'trulations," she said. "I know you will both be very happy."

Harker squirmed, not wanting to give anything away but was spared from saying anything by Olga.

"Thank you, Miss Mercy," the girl's smile was bright. "I'm sure we will be." She squeezed Harker's hand. "We both have big plans."

The doors behind them burst open and Olga's family walked in, followed by a chattering, cheerful crowd as the party began.

"Smile darling," Olga wrapped her hand around

Harker's arm. "The show is only getting started."

Harker groaned, letting her warm hands guide him toward her family to be kissed and shaken by the hand. It was going to be a long afternoon, but they would be heading out of town before the last rays of the sun had died. An open trail, a steady destination, and a determination to get this over with plastered a smile on his face as Harker made the rounds.

"That wasn't so bad, was it?" Olga asked hours later.

"I guess we survived," Harker agreed. "Are you ready to go?"

Olga sighed, turning back to her family. "Let me say goodbye."

∞∞∞

Olga kissed her family goodbye then turned toward the front door where Harker was preparing their conveyance. She smiled as Beau and Jude carried her bags to the front stoop. This trip was bound to be a big adventure. Perhaps she was silly to go through with the wedding, but if she was going to be an independent woman, why not have the fun of a fake marriage?

"You'll be safe?" her father asked, taking her hand as she waited for her new husband.

"We'll be safe, Papa," Olga smiled, seeing the worry in his eyes. "Harker is a good man. He's made his mistakes, but we all have." Olga felt her cheeks heat at the deception in her heart, but this was what she had to do. Then finally, Harker could get away, and she could return to Needful, a free and independent woman.

Phineas leaned in, kissing her cheek. "I'll keep you in my prayers."

Olga pulled her father close, hugging him as tears pricked her eyes. "I love you, Papa."

"Ready?" Harker's voice broke in as he came forward leading two saddle horses and a packhorse.

"Oh," Olga gaped at the animals. "Is that how we're traveling?"

"It's all I have," Harker said.

"All right." Olga took a deep breath, lifted her skirts and stepped forward. "You'll have to put me up. I'm not a very good rider."

Harker watched as Phineas gazed at him questioningly then stepped into motion. Taking Olga's hand, he led her to his stocky bay. "This is Bandit," he said. "He's a good horse. He won't give you any trouble."

"Good," Olga looked up at the man then squealed as he wrapped his hands around her waist and lifted her to the saddle, settling her sideways across the swells.

"You hold on here," he continued, wrapping her hands around the saddle. "Kindo will follow you an' you'll follow me."

"What's your horse's name?" Olga asked, still catching her breath.

"That's Scout," Harker smiled, turning to look at the leggy chestnut. "Don't worry." He turned back, looking into her downturned face. "Everything will be fine."

Olga nodded once, casting her eyes back to her father and offering him a bright if false smile and Harker turned, lifting his hand.

"I'll look after her sir," he said. "Despite what you think of me, I'd never let any harm come to your girl."

"You'd better not," Phineas said, taking one look at his second youngest child, then turning on his heel and disappearing into the boardinghouse.

"We'll make it to the Ferry tonight." Harker turned back to Olga. "We can stay there an' then carry on the next day." He half-smiled. "We'll be taking the main road an' can stay in a town or rest stop each night until we get to Houston."

"It's an adventure," Olga said, but her voice didn't hold the brightness it had a mere hour ago.

"Don't worry." Harker patted her knee. "We'll be fine."

Turning, he threw a leg over his horse and clicked, heading out of town.

A tiny 'eep' escaped Olga's lips and she heard Harker chuckle as the horses lurched into motion. She hoped the man was right.

The sky behind them was turning gold and orange as they rode out of Needful. It was a fair night, but Olga was thankful she'd grabbed her wrap when she had changed out of her pretty dress. As the sun set the night would grow cold.

"Are you sure we shouldn't take a train or a boat?" she called, adjusting her balance on the horse. She was wedged between the swells of the saddle horn and the cantle of the seat but still didn't feel completely secure.

"I don't like trains," the man ahead spoke, his voice husky. "If we were meant to travel that fast, the Good Lord would have given us wheels."

Olga didn't know if she should laugh or worry, but she decided to put her faith in Harker. The man had lived up to his part of the deal, and she would live up to hers.

"How long until we get to the Ferry station?"

"About three hours?"

"It will be dark." Olga couldn't keep the hint of worry from her tone.

"I've made the ride a few times," Harker replied. "Scout knows his way."

Olga looked down at the horse she rode. "And what about Bandit?"

"Bandit will go where ever Scout goes."

Olga twisted in the saddle, watching the other horse, a pale animal with dark main, trotting behind her. "They all stay together?"

"That's how I trained 'em," Harker replied. "I've spent a lot of time on the trails," he continued. "I need animals I can depend on. I can't have my horses wanderin' off now can I?"

"I hope not."

Harker pulled his horse to a stop and let Bandit come alongside. "I won't leave you behind, Olga."

Olga peered into the growing darkness at the man, still dressed in his suit. Her name on his lips sounded special, and she smiled, feeling a little more confidence return.

"Thank you. I didn't know this would be so difficult."

A warm hand grasped hers, where they held tight to the saddle horn. "We made a deal," Harker spoke, his voice close to her ear. "I don't go back on my word."

Something warm washed over Olga, and she found herself relaxing as Harker held her hand. "Thank you." She felt small yet strong with her smaller hand in his calloused one.

"Are you ready for an adventure?"

"Yes," Olga laughed, lifting her chin. "I'm going to see something new, and when I get back to Needful, I'll have something to tell."

"That's the spirit."

"Well, let's go," Olga laughed again. "We don't have all night, you know."

Harker's sharp bark of laughter filled the prairie, and the horses stepped out again. With him at her side, Olga was sure they would get to the Ferry with no trouble.

## Chapter 6

"What do you mean he's thrown a shoe?" Olga asked as darkness pressed in around her.

"Bandit has thrown a shoe," Harker grumbled. "Completely gone. Didn't you notice he was stepping funny?"

"No," Olga squinted at the man in the darkness. "How was I supposed to know?"

Harker ran a hand through his hair, a sure sign he was agitated. "Well, we can't keep riding like this. I can't have a lame horse, an' I don't have the equipment to pull the other shoes off."

"Would that help?" Olga peered into the darkness. "Why can't I ride Kindo?"

"Because," Harker sighed again, "Bandit would still have to carry the extra weight of your baggage an' supplies."

"Oh," the situation was getting clear with each question, and Olga tried to comprehend what came next. "What do we do next?" Her voice was soft as she stood next to Harker, the dark prairie stretching before her like an unfathomable sea.

"We'll make camp here for the night then go on into the Ferry tomorrow." Harker blew a breath through his lips, starting when Olga gasped.

"What do you mean camp here? We can't just, just, stop and sleep in the middle of nowhere."

"Why not?" Harker asked. "We have at least a little gear. You can have my bedroll."

"What will you do?"

"I've slept under the stars many a time." The deep rumbling chuckle made Olga feel a little better, but she was still worried.

"I've never slept outside in my life."

"There's a first time for everything," Harker laughed again. "I'll get a fire going then unpack so we can get some sleep. Tomorrow you can ride Scout an' I'll walk."

"That will slow us down, won't it?" Olga could hear the man moving around in the dark, but the moon wasn't up, and she could only make out shadows.

"We're movin' slow no matter what." The man's voice was hushed as he stripped the saddle off of Bandit. "This horse isn't winnin' any races on three shoes. We'll be lucky if he doesn't pull something hobbling like this."

"I'm sorry," Olga breathed. "Poor Bandit."

"It's not your fault." Harker huffed. "I checked shoes last week. I don't know how this could have happened."

More noises in the dark indicated that Harker was moving their gear around and then a match flared to life, and he lifted it, gazing around the tiny circle of light.

The match burned out, dropping them back into darkness and Olga blinked, her night vision obliterated by the tiny flame.

"You stay where you are," the man she had reluctantly wed chided. "I'll get things goin'."

Olga wrapped her arms around her waist, feeling her corset biting into her ribs as she shivered. Then, in the distance, a coyote yelped, and she froze, her eyes going wide. "What, what was that?"

"Just a coyote," Harker's voice seemed far away and Olga wanted him to hurry back, his presence a comfort in the darkness.

Another match flared and Olga could see the cowboy crouched over a small pile of leaves and dry grass. The flame caught, glowing a red ember in the kindling as Harker placed sticks on the stack.

"Thank goodness we're where there are trees and limbs to burn." Olga was squeezing herself tight now, holding her breath as Harker blew the fire into life.

"Wouldn't matter," Harker said, puffing on the fire and making it dance. "We could use dried cow patties if we needed to."

"Eww!" Olga wrinkled her nose. "That must be terrible."

"Nah," Harker chuckled, adding more twigs and then branches to his fire. "Once they're dried out, it isn't bad. Up north, where the buffalo are, folks use dried dung as fuel all the time. Hardly any trees out there at all." He beckoned Olga to the fire with a hand. "You sit here an' add wood a little at a time while I tend the horses an' get the bedroll ready for you."

Olga nodded, taking a seat on the upturned saddle he'd placed by the fire. The warm glow and cozy light dispelled much of her worry, and the sounds of the cowboy working behind her eased Olga's fears a little more.

"It's a good thing we had a big dinner," she mused. "I've never cooked over a fire before."

"I've done plenty." Harker's words were short. "It's easy to heat a can of beans or fry a bit of bacon.

If you're hungry, I can find some jerky. I usually keep some in my saddlebags."

"No, thank you." Olga shook her head. She was tired after a long day, and the fun and excitement of the afternoon had evaporated with the last rays of the sun. She added another branch to the fire, the circle of light expanding as the flames grew.

"There you go," Harker moved from the other side of the blaze where he'd laid his groundsheet and bedroll. "You'll be snug in that. I learned goin' cheap on a bedroll don't pay long ago."

Olga stirred the fire with a stick. "Are you sure we're safe?"

"Why wouldn't we be?" Harker's question was punctuated by the yip of a coyote and Olga jumped. "Don't worry," the man laughed, "I might not be a salty character like that Boden, but I can kill a varmint if I need to."

Olga let her shoulders relax. She was tired, and her mind turned over her decision to go through with this wedding and annulment plan. At the time, it had seemed like a bit of fun. She had money saved from her sewing and would enjoy going to Houston to see the sights. Now, the night pressed in on her, held at bay by the weak light of the fire, and she missed her father and sisters.

"Why don't you turn in?" Harker asked his voice

soft. "You'll feel better after a good night's sleep."

Olga stood making her way to the bedroll on the other side of the fire and peeling back the blankets. Her eyes lifted again and she met Harker's eyes. "You won't go anywhere, will you?"

"I'll be right here," the cowboy said, his handsome face serious. "I'll bring some more wood over, but I'll be here. Don't worry."

Olga slipped into the folds of the bedroll, pulling it up to her chin against the night's chill and promptly fell asleep.

Harker watched the girl for several minutes. She looked sweet and peaceful laying there and a smile tugged at his lips. He was sure in a pickle this time and could only count his blessings that she didn't want him for keeps.

Shaking his head, the cowboy turned, scanning the prairie for branches. A dark clump of trees swayed in the breeze, and he made his way toward it. This trip was supposed to be easy with stops in towns and at roadhouses, so he hadn't packed much in the line of grub. His battered coffee pot, tin plate, and cup were always with him, but how was he supposed to take care of this woman with nothing on hand?

Shaking his head, Harker gathered more firewood listening as an owl slipped almost silently through the night in search of prey. He'd been too long in Needful, gotten comfortable with three meals a day, easy saddle and stock horses, and a soft place to lay his head.

"I'm a traveler," Harker mused as he gathered wood. "I'm not made to stay in one place grubbin' out a livin'." He shook his head as he walked back to the fire, his eyes landing on the sleeping form. Olga was a perky one. She hadn't complained about not having a wagon or buggy to carry them to Houston. Instead, she had let him plop her on his horse and start toward the next nearest town. Not many women of his acquaintance were that forgiving.

A shadow passed overhead, making Harker duck and the hoot of an owl filled the night.

"Aah!" Olga sat up, blinking around her, eyes wide. "What was that?" Her voice caught in her throat and Harker knew she was afraid.

"Just an old owl." He spoke softly the way he might with a spooky horse. "You go back to sleep."

Olga rubbed nimble hands against her eyes. She looked weary. "I don't think I can." Lifting her eyes, she gave him a pleading look. "You'll sleep on this side of the fire, won't you?"

Harker raised a brow. "If that's what you want."

"It is." Olga's chin quivered as she put on a brave face. "This is very strange to me."

Harker hefted the saddle he'd been sitting on, added another branch to the fire and circled around to the girl. Choosing a spot a few feet from her, he plopped the saddle blanket on the ground then settled the saddle like a pillow at one end. "Good night," he offered, curling up on the only cover available. "I'll be right here."

Olga woke to a damp chill trying to sink into her bones and shivered, squirming as her corset dug into her ribs. She'd crawled into the bedroll fully clothed but was growing more uncomfortable by the minute. The fire had died down, a slight glow in the middle of deep darkness. A shiver ran over Olga and the sound of a coyote howling at the tiny sliver of moon froze her blood.

Only feet away, Harker slept, curled in on himself, with nothing but his long coat to keep him warm. The coyote howled again, this time answered back by its kin.

Olga climbed to her feet, huffing as the cold pressed in. Lifting the bedroll, she moved it to the cowboy's side then slipped back in, draping it slightly over his shoulder.

"What are you doing?" Harker's voice was husky with sleep.

"I'm cold." Olga didn't think she needed to say more.

"So you just crawl in with a man to keep warm?"

"Well." Olga spluttered. "Well, we're properly wed if anyone asks." Her voice grew small. "Besides, the coyotes are getting closer."

Harker chuckled, sleep muting his mind as he swung an arm around the girl and shifted the bedroll so they could share the warmth. "Go to sleep, Olga," he sighed as she snuggled close, resting her head against his chest.

Olga squirmed, trying to shift the pesky corset, so that she could get comfortable, but now it was pressing into her side where she leaned into the warmth of Harker.

"Stop squirming," the man's voice was soft but firm.

"I can't get comfortable," Olga used her free hand to tug at her undergarments.

A warm hand pressed into her lower back and Olga gasped as the strings of her corset unfurled.

"Better?"

Olga spluttered, her cheeks flaming but as she pulled a deep breath into her lungs, she had to admit it helped.

"Go to sleep," she grumbled, settling in as Harker chuckled. The man was scandalous and she wondered if her father had been right. Perhaps he had meant to take more than a kiss at the party.

Closing her eyes, she pushed the thoughts away. If that were the case, wouldn't the man be trying something now? Over the past two weeks, Olga had gotten to know Harker; at least she had thought so. He seemed a simple man with a desire to have no strings holding him back. Surely he wouldn't put himself in a situation where there was no way out.

Dropping her hand to the man's chest and feeling his warmth seep into her, Olga's mind whirred with questions. It was too late to turn back now, though. The path she had started was meant to be trod, and there was no easy way out. She would have to trust Harker enough to get them to Houston and procure the annulment that would set her free to live the way she pleased. Her mind stilled, and she slept.

Olga wriggled in her bed, something warm and strong wrapped around her shoulders.

"Good mornin'," a strong voice echoed and she jumped, sitting up to stare down at Harker, a blush bringing more heat to her cheeks.

"Good morning," Olga mumbled, separating herself from Harker's grasp.

The man chuckled, pulling his long legs out of the blankets and standing. "I'll get some coffee while you freshen up. There's a stream over there an' the trees have enough green to give you some privacy."

Olga's face flamed again, redder than a chilli pepper and twice as hot. "Thanks," she said, shaking out her skirts and hurrying toward the woods.

∞∞∞

Harker chuckled, watching the young woman hurry toward the woods. Her striped dress was rumpled but the bright pattern still stood out in the morning sun.

She was cute when she got embarrassed, and he knew he wouldn't be able to resist teasing her on this trip, at least a little.

He wondered what she would do if he kissed her again. Perhaps they were going to Houston to get an annulment, but a kiss now and then wouldn't do any harm. After her enthusiastic embrace at the altar, he couldn't blame himself for wanting another kiss.

The cowboy shook his head. No, kissing is what had gotten him into this mess, and as soon as he had his annulment, he'd put Olga on a train back to her family and be on his way.

Moving to his saddlebags, Harker pulled out his coffee pot. He'd get a nice brew going then put Olga on Scout and set out toward the Ferry station. Again the cowboy shook his head. Olga must have come through the station when she arrived in Needful. He'd heard that all four girls and their father had arrived by stage, making a special trip and an evening run to do so.

Pouring water from his canteen into the pot, Harker stoked the fire back to life and sat the pot on a rock. It was high time they got to the next town and got on with the business at hand.

The rustle of grass told him that Olga was coming back and he looked up smiling at her slightly bedraggled appearance. The woman dressed so pretty all the time it felt good to know that she wasn't perfect all the time.

"Is that coffee I smell?" Olga smoothed her dress coming to a stop before the fire.

"Comin' right up," Harker grinned.

"You do know your way around a campfire." Olga smiled, and it did something funny to his heart. For some reason, her simple praise hit Harker like a kick from a mule, and a big smile spread across his face.

"I've been cookin' over an open fire most of my life," he said, his chest swelling a little. "It's second nature."

"Well, let's just see how the coffee comes out before I pass judgment." Olga's eyes sparkled teasing in the bright light of day.

Harker poured her a cup, placing it in her small hands. "Sorry, there's no cream or sugar."

"That's alright," Olga grinned. "I stopped putting those in my coffee ages ago." She lifted the cup to her lips and grimaced.

"That bad huh?" Harker's heart fell.

"No, strong and hot, but good." She offered him another smile. "I often stay up late into the night sewing," she confided. "I tend to drink whatever's left in the pot when everyone has gone to bed."

"Drink up an' we'll hit the road," Harker grinned, that feeling of worth filling him again. She liked his coffee. Now that was something.

A short half-hour later, Harker helped Olga onto Scout's back. The chestnut cowpony was taller than Bandit, and she grasped the man's shoulders, steadying herself when he lifted her high.

"I feel so high up," Olga chimed. "You won't let me fall, will you?"

"I'll be right here at your side," Harker promised as a feeling of protectiveness washed over him. This girl had promised him his freedom, and he suddenly wanted to be sure she was safe. Harker Stevenson had never been responsible for anyone before. His whole life had been as carefree as he could make it, but now, he found himself with a wife, even if a fake one, to care for.

It was an odd feeling, leaving Harker both worried and excited. He had trusted Olga to keep her word, but she had also put her trust in him and for some reason, he wanted to prove himself worthy of that trust.

"We'll be in town by noon," the cowboy said, taking up the reins and leading Scout toward the road. "It will put us a day behind getting to Houston, but you can sleep in a real bed tonight an' fix yourself up nice like you always do."

"You like how I dress?" Olga's voice was cheery.

"You have some fine duds," Harker agreed. "So many women walk around in the same mousy things. Borin', dull, nothin' to catch the eye. You, you have flash."

A giggle tittered from Olga and Harker turned to look. "My sisters don't like my choice of clothing. I like things to make a statement."

"Well, you do a good job with that. Like them stripes you're wearin' now."

The girl looked down at the dress she was wearing. "This? I made this with the fabric used to decorate the town for Christmas." Olga leaned forward a bit. "Adele thought it was scandalous."

"I think it looks right smart."

"Thank you."

Harker grinned as Olga straightened in the saddle, her eyes seeking out the path ahead. It was plain that she appreciated his words, and he stuck out his chest as if he'd done something important.

The dust of the trail and the slow plod of the horses, matching Bandit's uneven pace, soon began to wear on Harker though, and he felt the chafe of his newly restrained life.

In the past, he would have had enough gear to put a new shoe on the bay pony and could have raced off to something new.

Casting his eyes up at the girl beside him, he wondered if this was what marriage did to a man.

## Chapter 7

Colbert's Ferry was about what you would expect from an intersection of transportation routes. Boats waited at a tributary to the more significant rivers further south, carrying items up and down to the town for sale.

A stagecoach carrying passengers from the Ferry to destinations further along in Texas hurried by, horses chafing at the bit to be away, while a burly driver held them in, at least until they reached the edge of town.

Colbert's Ferry was a station of commerce, trade, and transition. It was also the nearest river crossing to Needful and Harker had helped to drive cattle to the stockyards once or twice.

The tinkling of a lively tune from one of the saloons along the street caught the cowboy's ears, and he licked his lips, thinking of a cold beer or a shot of whiskey.

"I remember this place," Olga said, looking around from her perch on Scout's back. "We came through here on the way to Needful."

"Did you take a boat or the train?" Harker asked, his eyes scanning for the blacksmith's shop.

"No, we came by train and then caught the Butterfield stage from there, whatever that town was."

"That must have been quite a journey," Harker grinned. Stage travel was at best uncomfortable, and at times downright miserable.

"I think it helped that it was just the five of us." Olga grinned. "No one cared if you bounced onto them or knocked heads going over a big bump."

Harker chuckled, imagining the four girls and their father crammed into a coach. "That's the smithy over there," he said, pointing toward a dark shed at the corner of town. "I'll drop you off at the station an' you can get a room then I'll take Bandit an' get his shoe replaced."

"I'll get the rooms," Olga said, emphasizing the 's' on the end. "I've some money of my own."

Harker nodded, a strange prickling dotting his shoulders. He was the man. He should be paying. The cowboy shook his head, not wanting to argue. This whole situation was only temporary. He could put up with it a bit longer.

The Colbert House was grander than expected,

a two-story affair with lots of windows and a tall water tank at one end. It was snug and sturdy and Harker was sure Olga would prefer it to sleeping under the stars. A hot meal and warm bed would go a long way to boosting the girl's lively spirits, and they could set out fresh the following day.

"I'll see you in a bit," Harker grinned. "See if you can find out about a meal."

Olga nodded with enthusiasm; it had been a long day with nothing but coffee and jerky to sustain them. "Be careful," she called as she walked across the stoop and pushed open the door.

Harker watched the young woman walk into the house then turned his horses toward the blacksmith's shop. Hopefully, he wouldn't be long and Olga would have procured accommodation and food. Her parting words lingered in his mind, and he smiled, surprised at how nice it felt to have someone offer such care.

Olga stepped into the house, looking around for anyone who could let her have a room. A man in a dirty apron greeted her, and she smiled as she moved forward.

"I'm wondering if I can get two rooms?" she

asked, raising two fingers. Her eyes lingered on the dark-haired man. "One for me and one for," she swallowed her cheeks flushing. "One for my husband."

"Nope," the man wiped his hands on his apron.

"No? Why not?" Olga ogled.

"Only one room left. Of course, you can have that, but we ain't no fancy hotel here."

"Oh. Of course." Olga blinked a few times, letting everything filter into her tired brain. "I'll take that room then and meals if you have them."

"Meals we can do." The man tipped his head in the direction of a battered desk and pulled out a key. "Bags?"

"My husband will bring them."

"Name?"

"Olga Fortuna." Olga sagged, shaking her head. "I'm sorry. Olga and Harker Stevenson."

The man looked up, his dark eyes examining her. "You running away from home, are ya?"

"No!" Olga's eyes grew wide. "We only got married yesterday."

A sharp chuckle erupted from the squat-looking man and Olga cringed.

"You want me to take you to your room or you want coffee?"

"Coffee," Olga said, "and bread if you can. I'll wait on Harker before going to my, our room."

"Suit yourself."

Olga followed the man into a square, somewhat crowded dining area with tables crammed into every corner. The smell of greasy food and unwashed bodies tickled her nose, but she pushed it aside, following the man to a table.

The eyes of hard-looking men, dusty drivers, and hearty boatman followed Olga across the room to the table, and she dropped her eyes, feeling their gaze. She suddenly wished she had stayed with Harker. Surely these men wouldn't have stared at her if she had been accompanied by the lean cowboy with the deep gray eyes.

"I'll get you that coffee," her guide said. "We keep pretty busy here so's we got fresh biscuits if that will do?"

"Yes. Thank you." Olga's stomach rumbled as she took a seat, the long day catching up with her as her nerves jumped. She was alone in a strange place, and her only friend was somewhere out there, unaware of her circumstances. Olga hoped that none of the men in the room would approach her. She wasn't sure what she would say.

Shaking her head, she looked out the window, watching for Harker's approach. How long did it take to get a horseshoe replaced?

The man in the apron returned, placing a steaming mug of coffee on the table along with fresh biscuits, jam, and butter.

"Thank you," Olga smiled, wishing she wasn't seated alone at this table. Would men in this part of Texas and Oklahoma think she wanted their attention because she was on her own? A shiver ran down her spine, but she focused on the hot biscuits, keeping her eyes on her hands and not meeting the bold gazes of the men around her.

Harker gazed around him as men on horses, families in wagons, and other transport rumbled by. His hands fidgeted with the reins as he waited his turn at the smithy. Gray eyes flickered toward the tall two-story house, complete with a picket fence and tall water tower. He had heard that the railroad was planning to come through and were already working on a bridge upriver from the ferry. Texas would certainly grow after that.

Benjamin Franklin Colbert, a member of the Chickasaw Federation, had taken over the ferry business in 1826 and soon, it had become the primary crossing for anyone headed into Texas. The big house and farm had grown and soon, Colbert had begun renting out rooms in the two-story structure.

There had been a good deal of play back and forth across the ferry during the war, but now a peaceful, if hustling, commerce surrounded the area.

Harker knew that the going rate for cattle, horses, and men was ten cents per head and had helped move cows across the river several times since stopping in Needful. Now, all he wanted to do was get his horses settled and find Olga. Was she frightened being in the big house on her own? Was she able to get a room, and did she have enough money?

Thoughts whizzed through Harker's head, and he shook it, trying to slow his mind's pacing. He'd never worried about these things before. Olga was a free agent and certainly able to look after herself. Wasn't she?

A hard-eyed man in a battered gray uniform rode by on a slat-ribbed horse and Harker shivered. "How much longer?" he called to the blacksmith, fitting the shoe to Bandit's hoof.

"A lot faster if you'd stop distracting me," the broad-shouldered man shot back. The sound of a hammer tapping in a nail punctuated the words.

Harker ground his teeth with impatience as he told himself he was tired and on edge, but as soon as the smithy lowered Bandit's hoof, the cowboy paid him and turned to the stables. In mere minutes, his horses were stabled, and he grabbed Olga's bags, hurrying toward the Colbert House.

"You have a room for me?" Harker asked as he caught the eye of a stocky man in a dirty apron. "Harker Stevenson."

"Hmph," the man said, looking him up and down. "Your wife is in the dining room. I can take those bags to your room for two bits," he added, eyeing the bags.

Harker dropped the bags as a peal of laugher reached his ears and tossed the man a coin. "Thanks," he shot, hurrying into the next room where Olga's voice fluttered.

The dining room was crowded when Harker walked in, his gray eyes scanning the room for Olga. A group of cowboys crowded around one table, and he skipped by them looking for the woman he currently called wife.

"You're joshing," Olga's voice pulled Harker back to the group of men and he squinted, trying to find her in the crowd. "I've never heard the like."

"It's true," a deep voice echoed. "A catfish as big

as a pony, and he caught it with his bare hands."

Harker pushed his way toward the table, feeling a slow burn in his belly. Why were these men harassing Olga?

"Hello Dear," the cowboy drawled. "I was afraid you'd be worried without me." His eyes shot around the crowd and something hot seemed to chafe under his collar.

"Harker." Olga's eyes sparkled. "These gentlemen were keeping me company while I waited on you. Gentleman, meet Harker."

"Her husband," Harker grinned, baring his teeth like an angry dog.

"Nice to meet you." The crowd seemed to mumble as they began to disperse.

"Oh, they're leaving." Olga watched as the various men moved back to their tables.

"Good riddance," Harker hissed under his breath. He'd been worried that Olga would be scared and alone while he was gone, but instead, her pert face and cheerful nature seemed to have drawn men like bees to the honey pot.

"What was that?" Olga leaned over the table expectantly.

"Nothin'." Harker raked a hand over his face settling his nerves. "I was worried you'd be alone."

"Oh, everyone's been so nice," the girl grinned. "Biscuit?"

Harker looked down at a basket of fresh biscuits and sighed. "Thank you."

"You two eatin'?" the man in the apron returned, his dark eyes flicking between the couple.

"Yes, thank you." Olga smiled. "What do you have?"

"Chicken an' dumplings." The man's flat tone was not encouraging.

"That will do nicely," Harker said. "I know you're hungry, dear."

Olga blinked at him, surprised by the endearment then nodded. "I am."

In mere minutes two piping bowls of chicken and dumplings sat before them along with more biscuits and coffee. As Harker bit into the first real food he'd had since his wedding supper, he looked up, meeting Olga's eyes.

"Those men weren't botherin' you, were they?" he asked. "You weren't scared?"

Olga shook her head, her eyes locked on his. "No. At first, I didn't know what to say when they all started to introduce themselves to me."

"There aren't a lot of women in these parts," the lean cowhand said. "It's not surprisin' they would be drawn to a pretty thing like you."

Olga blushed, dropping her eyes to her bowl once more. "I'm afraid I have bad news," she said, lifting her napkin and twisting it in her hands. "They only had one room."

Harker let a slow breath out of his lungs. They would have to spend another night alone together, and he was suddenly pleased. At least he would know that Olga was safe from the unwanted attentions from the other guests. She would be safe with him, and he could see that nothing happened to the little seamstress at his side.

The room looked too small for both of them as Olga followed Harker inside. A small double bed, with a simple blanket over it, sat by a window and a cupboard stood against the far wall.

"It isn't much, is it?" the young woman asked.

"I've seen worse," Harker moved to the window on the far side of the room, pulling the curtain back and gazing outside. The ferry was docked on the other side of the river, and several wagons, along with men, women, and horses, were loading to make the crossing.

"I'm sorry," Olga said, shaking her head. "I didn't mean to complain."

Harker turned, letting the curtain fall. "I don't think I've heard you complain once," he mused. "You've held up well under the circumstances."

Olga shook her head. "I thought it would all be an adventure. Now, I'm not so sure."

"You haven't changed your mind, have you?" Harker's gray eyes bore into Olga's. "You aren't backin' out?"

"No!" Olga hurried across the room, placing her hand on his arm. "I'm not going back on my word. I still want the annulment as much as you do." The young woman dropped her eyes to her shoes. "It's just far more difficult than I thought it would be."

Harker placed a finger under her chin, lifting her face so he could look her in the eye. For the briefest second, he wanted to kiss her, pull her tight, and reassure her; possibly never let her go. But, with great effort, the cowboy pushed those nonsense thoughts away. "We'll make it," he grinned. "You'll see. The horses are in good shape, we have enough money, an' we'll pick up a few extra provisions in case of any more troubles."

Olga's bright smile punched Harker in the heart and the glimmer in her eye made him lick his lips.

"Thank you," she said. "I'm glad you feel so confident. I think that as long as I'm with you, I won't worry."

Harker dropped his hand, where it still rested under Olga's chin. Something deep inside seemed to stir to life, and he savagely shoved it back down. A sense of protectiveness bubbled just under the surface, and he knew that if he didn't watch his step, things could change between him and his little bride.

"I'll step out while you get ready for bed," Harker spoke, striding to the door.

Olga watched the man leave and sighed. Her plan had seemed easy when they were back in the safety of Needful. But now, she wasn't so sure. Her dark eyes flickered toward the door, and she thought about the man she was on this journey with. For some reason, she felt comfortable with him. He never seemed to let anything bother him. Well, perhaps the wedding, but now he seemed confident and able.

Olga slowly unbuttoned the line of buttons down her back. After two days in the same dress, it was looking travel-worn. Finally, after several minutes of struggle, she managed to get all but one button undone.

She considered popping the button off, but then she might tear her dress. With the dress shop just starting, and with Beth as a partner, Olga couldn't afford to damage even one of her many dresses.

"Harker," she called her hands still behind her back. "Could you come in, please?"

∞∞∞

Harker opened the door stepping in and closing it. He'd heard Olga call him and was sure she must be snuggled up in the bed, preserving her modesty. But, when he lifted his eyes and saw the young woman standing there, a wide expanse of shiny corset exposed under her hands, he swallowed hard, spinning on his heel as he tried not to look.

"Could you just get this last button?" Olga twisted her head, looking over her shoulder. "It seems to be stuck."

"I don't think that would be appropriate," Harker said, his eyes fixed on the door.

"But I can't get it unhooked," Olga pleaded. "If I were back in Needful, Heidi or one of the Hampton girls would help. You're all I have."

Harker felt his will sag. She sounded so desperate. Closing his eyes, he walked toward where she stood, his hands fumbling before him.

"Oh, that tickles," Olga jumped at his touch.

"Here, the button in the middle."

Harker opened one eye peering at the young woman's back. She had just enough meat on her bones to make her a good armful, and he knew from the night before that she was warm and soft. Swallowing hard, he unhooked the button, stepping back as the pretty striped dress fell, pooling on the floor at Olga's feet.

"Oh my," Olga gushed, wrapping her arms around her middle. "I'm so sorry."

A bright splash of red tinged her cheeks as she stood before him in her shammy, corset, and pantaloons.

Harker's eyes widened, running the length of the woman. She looked fine. Too fine. Spinning on his heel, the man marched to the door, pulled it open and stepped outside. "I'll be back shortly," he called, hurrying down the stairs and out of sight.

Harker rolled his hands into fists as he raced down the stairs. He wanted to feel the smooth fabric of the young woman's corset under his fingers, and he growled, trying to put the thought out of his mind.

"Where can a man get a drink around here?" He asked as he hit the bottom floor.

"Ask in the dining hall," the man in the apron said. "They'll find you something."

Harker nodded his belly turning over as visions of Olga Fortuna, the girl he had wed, flashed before his eyes. Hopefully, he would wash the picture away with a nice cold beer. Maybe a round of cards would get his mind off of sharing a room with the pert little thing.

Harker ran a hand over his face, nodding to the same man in the apron from earlier, as he flopped into a seat. "Can I get a beer?" he asked. "Tall an' cold if you have it."

The man nodded, hurrying into another room and returning with a mug of beer.

In moments, Harker had down that one and asked for one more. He needed something to steady his nerves before he faced Olga again.

Two hours later, with darkness heavy on the house, Harker made his way back to the room, easing through the door as silent as a cat.

Stepping out of his boots, he made his way to the bed and climbed under the covers. A warm body snuggled close and the mellow feeling from a couple of drinks dissipated in an instant. Closing his eyes, Harker let Olga wriggle close with only a sigh. It was going to be a long night. Thoughts of that first stolen kiss teased at the edge of his mind, and the man tried to push them away.

Why did this girl have such an effect on him?

He'd kissed pretty girls before. Kissed them and rode away, but this time, it was different. She was so open, so full of life, and yet so vulnerable. Harker doubted the girl even knew the kind of danger she might be in if he were a different sort of man.

Blowing a breath through his lips, he opened his eyes and studied the ceiling above. Was this what people were looking for when they wed? A warm bedmate, someone to talk to, a body to travel with? His mind turned back to his mother and his heart pinched.

No, marriage was not for Harker Stevenson. He didn't need to fall in love only to have his heart ripped out of his chest.

His eyes dropped to Olga's head resting over his heart and he wondered if she would ever do something like that. She was such a sweet, sassy thing. She hadn't argued over any of his arrangements, but would time and the hardships of life change her?

Harker tried to push the thoughts away, but the more time he spent with Olga, the more he liked her, and the more he liked her, the more his life seemed lonely.

"Once I'm back on the trail, it will fade," he whispered to the empty room. "I'll be free as a bird, an' Olga will be nothin' but a funny tale, a memory to smile at on a cold night."

The girl stirred in his arms, and he tightened his grip instinctively. Her warm curves pressed against his side and Harker felt something new. Possessiveness was not the norm for him, but there it was, just like before in the dining room. Harker had wanted nothing more than to push every man in there away from the sweet Olga and her pretty dresses.

An owl called from across the river and Harker relaxed. This mess would all be behind him in a couple of days. He would get the girl to Houston, get an annulment, and be on his way to somewhere new and exciting. He traveled alone. He traveled light and he traveled fast. A woman would only be a hindrance.

Sleep finally claimed Harker, and he drifted into a troubled slumber. His weary mind traveling a dark empty trail as he sought something he could never find. As the final track ended in darkness, Harker started awake, jarring Olga, who slept tucked close to his side.

"Are you all right?" Olga sat up, the blanket falling away from a soft flannel nightgown with hash-like clusters on it. "Oh, my," she gasped. "You'll think me very forward sleeping so close."

"You didn't do anything wrong." Harker's voice was soft, weary. "I was dreamin' that's all."

"I take it you did not have a pleasant dream."

Harker sat up leaning against the headboard and turning to look at the young woman, his gray eyes full of doubt. "I was alone," he finally spoke.

"You're alone often, aren't you?" Olga looked him square in the face, not flinching at his dark look.

"I guess." Harker ran his hands through his hair. "I'm usually goin' somewhere, though." He shook his head, dropping his hands onto the blanket. "This was different. I was looking for someone or something an' could never find it. I'd come to the end of the trail an' there was nothin' there, only darkness."

Olga reached down taking Harker's hand in hers and the man dropped his gaze, studying the nimble fingers in the gray light of dawn. "Well, you're not alone right now." The girl giggled and her warm hands pressed into his. "I'm with you at least for a bit longer."

Harker ran a thumb over the girl's fingertips, feeling tiny prickles over the soft skin.

"Your hands aren't rough but your fingers are," he mused.

"That's from sewing." Olga tried to pull her hand away but Harker lifted it, studying the palm and finger pads. "I use a needle and thread constantly and handling fabric makes your fingers tough."

"I didn't know," Harker turned, offering Olga a soft smile.

"Why would you?" The girl shook her head. Her hair hung in a long braid over her shoulder and his fingers itched to lift it, feeling the silk tresses on his skin. "You don't sew, do you?"

Harker chuckled, shaking his head then noting the teasing light in Olga's eyes. "No, but my hands are hard an' calloused from workin' a rope or brandin' iron. They probably feel rough to you."

"They don't." Olga looked down at their hands once more. "They feel nice."

Harker gently placed the girl's hand back on the blanket then turned to get out of bed. "We'd better get ready," he said, feeling something thick in his throat. If he was going to get her to Houston and get an annulment, another night like this might ruin it all. Olga was sweet, sassy, warm and very attractive to him right now.

Keeping his back to the woman, he stepped into his pants, buckling the belt tight around his waist and reached for his shirt. "I'll meet you downstairs for breakfast."

A moment later, Harker was hurrying down the stairs of the Colbert House, his chest tight as he tried to get the vision of Olga out of his mind. The girl would be his undoing if he wasn't careful, and she had not one clue to her charms.

## Chapter 8

"Only one more day's ride an' we'll be there," Harker called back, making Olga look up from where she slumped in the saddle. She was tired after days of travel along dusty, poorly kept roads.

"Are you sure we couldn't have traveled by boat or rail?" she asked, brushing dust from her skirt.

"I don't like leavin' my horses behind," Harker replied. "Is it too hard for you? We can pitch camp an' have a rest if you'd like."

"No," Olga shook her head. "I'll be fine. I'm just tired of dust and horse, and well," she wiggled gingerly on the seat. "My padding does not protect me from a saddle, apparently."

Harker's chuckle caught her by surprise and Olga looked up as the man pulled rein. "Why don't we get down an' walk a while?"

Olga nodded, letting the cowboy dismount before reaching for him. They had done this so often now it was second nature for her to place her hands on his shoulders and let him lift her down.

"Maybe we could rest a spell," Olga finally spoke, her hand straying to her small bustle.

Harker nodded. "We'll rest up in that grove of trees," he offered. "Give the horses a chance to graze an' maybe eat something."

"Do we have any biscuits left from the last road stop?" Olga's stomach rumbled and she blushed with embarrassment.

"I think so. That woman that ran the place buttered a few for us an' wrapped them up." Harker lifted his head, examining the sky. "It's long about lunchtime already."

Olga took the man's arm as her tired legs wobbled under her and together, they moved into a thick clump of cottonwoods. A cheerful brook, filled by the spring rains burbled merrily beside them.

"Oh, this is lovely." Olga sighed, leaning against a tree. She had no desire to take a seat on one of the large rocks along the stream.

"Do you want me to make some bacon?"

"No," Olga looked up, offering an appreciative smile for Harker's offer. She knew he was being solicitous, so that they could get this annulment nonsense over with.

Harker turned, Olga's eyes following him as he

pulled biscuits from his saddlebags and hefted the canteen from the horn. "Hold this, while I loosen the girths an' let the horses rest."

Olga took the offered food and turned to gaze around her at the beautiful spot. The stream raced along behind a line of thick trees, patches of green grass springing up along the shore and around the rocks. The sound of the brook was soothing, and she breathed deeply of the fresh smell of wet earth, grass, and clean water.

"What's that?" she asked, tipping her head toward the road. A steady thrumming noise was growing louder, and Olga turned to peer through the branches at the dusty road.

"Shh," Harker's hiss was harsh and shocking, but Olga complied. The man's eyes darted toward the road, where a cloud of dust was growing ever closer.

"Olga," his deep whisper beckoned as he waved her toward him and the horses at his back. "Hold tight to the reins," Harker added, rummaging in his saddlebags for a spyglass.

"What is it?" Olga felt her stomach quiver at the look on Harker's face.

A finger across his lips hushed her and Olga's hands grew clammy around the leather she squeezed in a death grip.

Harker lifted the glass to his eye tracking the oncoming horses as the sound of galloping hooves grew louder. "Bushwackers," the wrangler hissed, stuffing the glass back into his bags and dragging his horses close. "Put your hand over Bandit's nose." The man's eyes darted between Olga and the road as the thunder vibrated the ground where they stood.

A low nicker rose in Bandit's throat but Olga stroked his nose, willing him to be quiet. A moment more and the riders dashed by, horses heaving and white with foamy sweat. Then, as the dust cloud faded, a loan rider charged forward, his weary mount stumbling and falling with a terrified scream.

Olga bit her knuckle, eyes wide as the boy atop the horse tumbled to the hard ground and lay still.

Harker's hand hovered over the pistol on his hip as the horse struggled to its feet and staggered a few feet, shaking the dust of the road from its back.

"He's just a boy," Olga's voice was so low she wondered if Harker could hear.

"He's a Bushwacker, like the rest." Harker's lips were next to her ear, his breath tickling her neck.

"Is he dead?"

The body in the road stirred as the dust cloud

made by the other riders swept on over the next hill.

"No." Harker rested his hand on the pistol at his hip as the boy stirred, rolling to his side, blood and dirt sticking to his face.

"I thought Quantrill's men had been defeated," Olga said. "Didn't they disband on his death in '64?"

"Yes," Harker's eyes stayed on the body in the road. "Much of his group, including the James brothers, created their own gangs though."

"You think that's what they are? But he's..." Olga turned her dark eyes full of concern. "He's no more than a boy. Thirteen at best."

"He's probably a war orphan with nowhere else to go."

"Can't we help him?"

Harker stared down at the girl next to him. Her eyes were full of pleading compassion and his heart pinched.

"That boy could be a killer," he argued. "We're best leavin' him there or take him to the law in

Houston."

"His horse doesn't look so good," Olga whispered. "Do you think it broke its leg?"

"I can't tell from here."

"Please," Olga's voice drove like a dagger to his heart. "Please, can't we help?"

Harker dropped his eyes, his shoulders sagging as he felt something inside him break. No one had been there to help him or his father when his ma had left. They'd been two heartbroken souls alone with no way to help each other or themselves.

"If he tries anything, I'll shoot him." Harker's voice sounded sharp as he pulled his pistol from the leather on his hip. "Hold tight to the horses," the cowboy continued. "We can't afford to lose them if he tries anything."

"Hello," Olga's voice was soft in the warm day and Harker cringed as she moved around him toward the body in the road. "Can we help you?"

The boy shot upright, his bloody face and wide eyes making him cringe.

"Get away," the boy cried. Blood trickled over his forehead and he blinked it away.

"We're not here to hurt you," Olga spoke.

Harker crowded close, his hand steady on the

pistol at his side.

"Why's he got a gun then?" The boy's truculent voice broke as he lifted an arm, wiping blood from his eyes so he could see. "He's gonna shoot me."

"Harker will not shoot you," Olga said, her lips twisting with disgust. "Not unless you decide to do something stupid."

"You leave me alone," the boy's obstinate tone weakened further. "The fellas will be back for me soon. You'll see."

"Those riders aren't comin' back for you," Harker spoke, his voice steady. "An' if you don't want a necktie party comin' on you quick, you'll come with us."

"Please," Olga took a step closer, and Harker moved to keep the boy in his line of sight. "We'll help you. At your age, I can't imagine you've done anything so terribly wrong. You could go home."

"I ain't got a home." Again, the boy sniffed, this time running his sleeve under his nose. "Everything I called home is gone."

"Then we can find you a new one," Harker said. "But you'd best get up an' come along with us." His gray eyes flickered to Olga. "Fetch the horse, Olga."

Olga nodded, not offering a wit of argument. "Can he stand?" She spoke to Harker, indicating the boy.

"I can stand." The wheedling defiance returned. Getting his tattered boots under him, the boy struggled to his feet, swaying slightly as Harker stepped to his side.

"Through those trees," Harker said, keeping the boy before him. "No funny business."

"What's your name," Olga asked, giving Harker a stern look. "You don't look more than twelve or thirteen."

"I turned thirteen on my last birthday." The boy's voice was a harsh rattle.

"And when was that?" Harker's hard eyes bore into the boy with a knowing glare.

"Last week." The boy hung his head, tripping toward the grove of trees as the distant sound of horses galloping along the road tickled their ears. "I told you they'd come back for me."

"If I judge right," Harker looked back down the road the way they had come. "That's a posse hot on the trail of the gang you were with. If you want a short end to your short life, I'd try flaggin' them down."

The boy lifted his head, seeing the dust cloud sweeping toward them, and he swallowed hard, his bony Adam's apple bobbing in his skinny throat.

"Hurry up," Olga urged, leading the limping horse behind her. "If they catch you, we'll all be in trouble."

Harker pointed toward the trees, and the boy moved, the cowboy close behind, and Olga straggling behind with the lame horse.

"Now," Olga stopped at the tiny encampment. "Tell me your name and sit down there like a civilized human being."

"Rob." The boy swiped beneath his nose again as a drop of blood spattered from his cheek to his shoulder.

"We need to get him out of those bloody clothes," Olga hissed at Harker. "If that is a posse and they find him, they'll hang him for sure."

"I didn't do nothin' worth hangin'." Rob lifted his chin, his tattered face already bruising.

"The question is, what did the others do?" Harker's gray eyes pinned the boy to the stone he had settled on.

Rob swallowed hard but didn't speak. The raids against settlers and townsfolks alike ranged from theft to murder. "They said they were raidin' a storehouse."

"I hope that's all," Olga said. "Now give me that shirt and go wash up in the stream. Harker," her eyes roamed over the tall, lean cowboy. "Can you get him one of your shirts? It will be too big but it will have to do."

Harker flicked his eyes between Olga and Rob then nodded. "You keep an eye out."

Olga hurried to her packs on Kindo and rummaged for a clean strip of fabric. "You need to get that dirt out off your cheek," she said, moving toward the boy. "Let me help."

"I don't need no help." Rob spat, splashing more water on to his face. "My ma's gone, an' I don't need some prissy woman fussin' over me."

The clout to the back of his head caught the boy by surprise, and he fell face-first into the creek bed, barely catching himself on his hands.

"What'd you do that for?" he sat up, glaring and rubbing the back of his head.

"Your mama would have done the same if I'm any judge," Olga said. "Now hush up and do as you're told."

A flicker of something flashed in the boy's pale blue eyes, but a hint of hope seemed to glimmer on the edges. Olga dipped the rag in the stream and began cleaning the debris from the boy's face as gently as she could. Each flinch and hiss of pain told her it wasn't gentle enough, but it had to be done.

Splashing downstream drew Olga's attention and she looked up to see Harker leading the lame horse into the stream where he began wiping it down with cold water.

Harker looked up, his eyes meeting hers as he smiled. "If that posse comes our way, they'll wonder why one of our horses is all lathered up but the other three are fine." He nodded toward his three horses, contentedly nibbling grass by a pool. "Plus, this might help with that pulled tendon. I'm afraid this horse isn't going anywhere fast for the next few days."

Olga returned to her work, holding Rob's chin in her firm grasp. "This is going to need a stitch," she said, shaking her head. "I'll get my needle and thread." Her dark eyes dropped to the boy's blue ones as she released his chin, the last flex of rock removed from the abrasion that now flowed freely with a crimson flood. "Can you take it?"

"I can take it." The boy's bravado returned.

"Finish washing and get that shirt on." Olga could hear riders approaching at a good pace. Bandit lifted his head and whinnied as the silence of the glade ended in a rumble of shouts.

"Hello the camp!" a male voice echoed through

the trees. "Who goes there?"

"Ride on in," Harker replied. "We know what you're lookin' for."

Olga turned, looking at Rob, whose eyes went wide with fright.

∞∞∞

Olga felt her heart start to race at Harker's words. Would he turn the boy over to the posse, possibly costing him his life? She tried to reassure Rob with a sickly smile, but her heart wasn't in it.

Three riders made their way through the trees as Harker's horses lifted their heads, nickering low in greeting. Each man had their eyes on the small party, and the glint of rifles already in their hands made Olga swallow hard.

"Who are you?" A swarthy man with a long mustache asked, his eyes traveling to Harker. "What are you doing here?"

"Harker Stevenson," the cowboy spoke. "My wife, cousin an' I are travelin' to Houston. The boy's horse stumbled an' fell with him, so we stopped here to rest a spell."

"You see anyone else ride by?" Another man spoke.

"Yes," Harker shook his head. "We kept hid an' quiet too. It looked like a band of bushwhackers or raiders to me."

"That they are," the man with the mustache spoke, turning his horse to get a better look at the camp. The afternoon light glinted off of the badge on his chest and his hard eyes returned to Harker. "You see which way they went? First, they raided a storehouse back in town, stole supplies and what money was on hand. Then, hit the storekeeper over the head. It's a good thing he'll be all right."

Both Harker and Olga pointed along the road.

"They were ridin' hard," Harker said. "I don't think you'll catch 'em."

"We'll catch them," the man with the badge said, quiet confidence oozing in his words. "Maybe not tonight, but we'll catch them, in time."

Olga's eyes flickered to Rob, who sat hunched by the stream, eyes studying the water as it flowed.

"You stayin' here for the night?" the lawman asked.

"Depends on the horse," Harker answered. "It's pretty lamed up."

The lawman's dark eyes pinned Harker and he felt his heart drop. If this hard-bitten harbinger of the law suspected him of keeping a fugitive, he would come down hard on all of them, including Olga. An old prayer raced through his mind, unbidden and for the first time since he was a boy, Harker turned to God for help.

"I'll check in with you if we ride back this way," the man with the badge spoke one last time. "Make sure you're alright." His dark eyes came to rest on Rob for the long count of a heartbeat, and then he reined his horse around, waving his rifle for the others to follow and galloped back out to the road.

"You didn't turn me in." The boy's voice was barely audible above the sound of the babbling brook. "I thought you'd let them take me."

Harker turned on the boy. "I probably should have turned you over." His words were hard, but an edge of something more tinged them. "You've been ridin' with bad men, who have done bad things. You should have to answer for your crimes."

"All I did was hold the horses," the boy choked. "I never hurt no one."

"But you would have," Olga stepped in, a needle and thread in her hands. "In time, if you had stayed with them, you would have hurt someone. You've been given a second chance," she continued, her eyes lifting to Harker's as her heart turned. "I hope you'll make the best of it."

Rob looked between the two of them. "Why are

you helpin' me?"

"Because you're one of God's creatures." Harker was the first to answer. "The Good Lord believes in second chances, an' we should too."

Olga's bright smile hit Harker in the chest, and he almost took a step back from the blow. The light in her dark eyes was blinding as he realized that his whole life he had spent running from himself.

"Thank you." The young woman's words drifted into Harker's soul and something caged woke, lifting its head to the fresh new light of love.

"Let me see about that cut," Olga turned, hustling toward Rob, her needle glinting in the sun. "This is going to hurt," she added, setting her jaw with determination.

Harker watched the young woman bustle away, her skirt swishing with every step. She hadn't turned her back on the boy. Maybe he could convince her that freedom wasn't being alone or on your own. Independence could prove to be no more than loneliness.

Thoughts of Needful, a steady job, and Olga's sweet smiles fluttered through his head, and Harker wondered how he had ended up here.

This journey had been to freedom, a trip to Houston to garner an annulment from a marriage neither party wanted. Now, he wanted nothing more than to see that light of acceptance and understanding in Olga's eyes for the rest of his life.

# Chapter 9

"What do we do now?" Olga finished stitching the deepest cut by Rob's eye then twisted to look over her shoulder at Harker.

"You up for stayin' here tonight?" Harker asked. "I know we planned on stoppin' at the stage depot outside of Houston, but..." He looked around him, his eyes lingering on the boy.

"We can stay." Olga looked at Rob. "You won't cause any trouble, will you?"

The boy shook his head, despondent.

"This horse couldn't carry him if he wanted to run," Harker said, lifting the slat ribbed, dark bay's front hoof. "He has a pulled tendon."

"I'll get our things from the horses," Olga said with one last backward glance at Rob. "We'll all need a good night's rest."

Moving to the horses, Olga untied the bedroll from Harker's saddle. It looked like it would be another night of roughing it. She didn't like it, but the boy wasn't fit to travel on his own, and she didn't trust him not to try to find that band of outlaw renegades.

Fiddling with the knots of the arroyos, Olga studied Harker, who was examining the weary horse's leg. His hands were gentle as he prodded the swelling, and he shook his head, sighing. Olga knew those hands were warm, strong, and able. She remembered the first night they had slept out under the stars, and his deft loosening of her corset.

A blush tinged the young woman's face, and she forced those admittedly pleasant thoughts away. She didn't like to be such a bother to the man. Obviously, he wanted to be rid of her, but the more she grew to know him, the less she wanted to part.

Harker had a quick wit, a keen eye, and he never left her feeling afraid.

Olga shook her head, trying to dispel her silly notions. In another day, they would ride into Houston, find the right judge and part ways.

"What do I call ya?" Rob's weak voice drifted from the stream. "You know my name, but I don't know yours."

"I'm Olga," Olga replied. "This is Harker." She blushed, wanting to add 'my husband' to the introduction but held her tongue.

"You're headed to Houston?"

"Yes." Harker led the horse from the stream letting the animal pick its way carefully onto the grass.

"Is that where you're from?"

Olga pulled the bedroll from the saddle and carried it to a grassy area near the stream. "No, we're from Needful."

"Where's that?" Rob looked between the two of them. "I never heard of it."

"New town," Harker grumbled, picking up a rock. "Why don't you make yourself useful an' help me get a fire goin'?"

Rob struggled to his feet, swaying slightly then growing steady. "I'll get wood."

"Don't go far." Olga and Harker both barked at the same time.

"He won't try to run away, will he?" Olga hurried to Harker's side.

"Not with that posse out there, at least not if the boy has any sense."

Olga let out a breath she didn't know she had been holding. "He's so young."

"You can't be that much older," Harker teased.

"Seven years makes a big difference."

Harker chuckled. "You're a real woman of the world."

Olga swatted at the man and together, they broke into laughter, dispelling the tension that had permeated the space since the posse had arrived.

"What can I do?" Olga finally asked.

"Nothin' yet," Harker dropped a hand to her shoulder, giving it a gentle squeeze. "I'll get a fire ring set up an' we'll make some food." He nodded toward the boy gathering firewood. "He looks like he should eat."

Olga nodded, "I'll try to help."

Within half an hour, the trio had a small fire and camp in place. Bacon sizzled in Harker's small pan and a pot of coffee simmered on a stone. Olga could hear Rob's stomach rumble halfway across the meadow and handed him a biscuit to nibble while they waited on their food.

"What will you do with me when you get to Houston?" Rob asked. His blue eyes darted between Olga and Harker like a wary animal.

"That's up to you." Olga flicked her eyes to Harker then back to the boy. "You can go home."

"I don't have a home."

"Plenty of people don't have a home no more," Harker said. "That doesn't mean they can't make a new one. Every day a man has to decide as to how he'll live. He can give up, turn bad, run away, or" Harker turned, his gray eyes falling on Olga and her breath caught in her chest. "Or start something new."

Olga couldn't look away from Harker's handsome face. There was something different about the way he looked at her. A question in his eyes, and it plucked at her heartstrings. Was the man reconsidering the annulment? Was he willing to return to Needful and start fresh as her husband?

Butterflies fluttered in her stomach and Olga wondered what it would be like to be married in more than name. What would Harker do in Needful? Would he continue to work for the various ranches? Would they have to live in the boardinghouse forever? She shook her head, chasing away the ridiculous thoughts. Harker had made it plain that he wanted no strings on him.

"You see," Harker's voice continued as he dished up the bacon. "A man isn't a man until he takes responsibility for his actions. One simple, playful moment in his life can change everything, an' he can either run from it or stand up an' make the most of what he's been offered."

Olga's mouth went dry as the words slipped into

her soul. "Harker Stevenson, what are you trying to say?"

Harker looked down at the fire, lifting a hand to scratch behind his ear then met her gaze. "I'm sayin' I might could use a real home."

"You mean it?" Olga's heart fluttered, her hand rising to cover her chest.

"I do. If you're willin'."

Olga walked back to the fire, sitting on a rock next to Harker. "What will this mean for me?"

"Whatever you want it to."

Olga's mind reeled, thinking about what the man was saying. She had only known him for a few weeks, and other than his ability to make her laugh and get her into a serious predicaments, she knew little about him.

"I don't want to give up my shop."

"Why would you need to?" Harker's eyes met hers.

Olga watched the man as he studied the boy who had taken his food and moved over with the horses. "I don't know," she finally said.

Harker turned back to look at her, handing her a small plate with bacon and biscuits. "That boy back there. The one you rescued an' want to see safe an' sound, he an' I have a few things in common."

Olga turned, looking at the boy who was stroking Kindo's neck. "Like what?"

"When I was about his age, my mother left. No word. No indication. Nothing. She just left. My father was a farmer. He worked hard to make ends meet, but nothin' was ever good enough for my ma. They argued all the time. They fought over every little thing. My pa was a good, honest, hard-workin' man, but it wasn't enough. I guess I wasn't either because she left. A few years later, my father got sick an' died. The day they buried him, I climbed on a horse an' never looked back. I've been a wanderer ever since. I don't take well to bein' held in one place, an' I never looked twice at a woman. Not seriously anyway."

Olga blushed and the man offered her a smile as he continued with his story.

"My pa might have gotten some sickness an' died of it, but it was a broken heart that killed him. I knew it even if no one else could see it. I swore I'd never let a woman make me feel that way. I wouldn't put my heart in a vice like that."

"But now?" Olga felt her heart racing at the man's words. Men back home had never paid much attention to her. Many of them laughed at her fashion choices or teased her about the bright colors and loud patterns she chose. Even coming to Needful, Olga had never dreamed of romance or pretty words, but what Harker was saying now dove straight to her heart. He was trusting her with his heart and something warm and squishy seemed to bloom in her soul.

"Now, I'd like to see what we could be. You lived up to your promises an' your bargain. I know part of it was a lark for you, but it could be more." Harker's voice faded, his gray eyes boring into hers.

"Why?" Olga shook her head. She knew Harker couldn't love her, despite his pretty words and that sizzling kiss. "What changed?"

Harker nodded toward the boy, who was now examining his horse's damaged leg. "I could have ended up like that boy. Lost, alone, angry. I lost everything long before the war, an' I never joined up on either side. I had nothin' worth fightin' for an' just kept movin', keepin' away from it all. I've never lacked for work an' never needed much. It was easy. All I had to care for was myself." Harker's gray eyes grew sad and he reached for Olga's hand. "I didn't realize that I wasn't only alone. I was lonely. These past few weeks, this trip, it's shown me how nice it is to have someone around who cares for you."

Olga smiled, squeezing his hand. "I think I

understand. I know I'm no great beauty, and most men don't like my sense of fashion. My sisters call it a fixation, but I love clothes, even if I have to buy the most outlandish patterns to afford better fabric."

Harker raised a brow and Olga shook her head.

"What I'm trying to say," Olga continued. "Is that no one ever paid attention to me like you have. You make me laugh, you even like my clothes. I've never once felt like an outsider with you." The young woman dropped her eyes, but Harker's warm grip made her lift them again.

"You're a lovely young woman." He smiled, his eyes bright. "An' I like all the pretty things you wear. You never wear any of those borin' gray things an' the patterns stand out. I'm sick to death of women all dressed the same. Same gray, black, or white everything."

Olga blinked at the man. Most of the women of Needful wore simple things, but in a wide array of colors.

"Harker, what color is my skirt?" she asked, looking down at the bright pink dress covered in thin black pinstripes.

"Gray with black stripes," the man answered. "I like them stripes. They show off your figure."

Olga felt her cheeks heat again but she shook her

head. "My dress is pink."

Harker ran a hand through his hair, blowing a breath from his cheeks. "That's why I like your duds," he admitted, a sheepish grin on his face. "I can't pick out colors so good."

Olga smiled as the revelation hit her. "You're color blind."

Harker shrugged. "I guess so. All I know is that most things look the same."

A giggle filled Olga's chest and she shifted closer to Harker. "You're an exceptional man," she said. "I think that we could try to see how things go between us."

A bright grin spread across the man's face, and he leaned forward, placing a sweet kiss on her lips.

"Ugh," Rob's sound of disgust made them break apart, laughing. "I hope I ain't gonna have to put up with that all day. I'd rather take my chances with that posse."

Laughter echoed over the small clearing as Harker wrapped an arm around his girl.

## Chapter 10

"The way I see it," Harker stood over the dead fire two days later, "is you can come back with us or head home." The man swallowed hard, looking over at the mounts. "You can take Kindo an' I'll have your horse in exchange if you chose to leave."

"You can't be serious?" Rob gaped. "You'd give me a fine horse like that?"

"If it meant you got home safely, yes." Olga chimed in. "We discussed it last night, and we're headed back to Needful to start a new life. You're welcome to come with us or leave." The young woman twisted her hands together with doubt and Harker draped his arm around her shoulders.

"What would I do in this Needful? Sounds like a silly name for a town."

"Olive Hampton named the town." Olga bristled. "She was overheard saying the place was in need of good women."

"You could work with me," Harker said with a chuckle at Olga's outburst. "I'll go back to my job with Anderson as a wrangler an' teach you to work cattle. Then, later you can do as you please."

"Where will I stay?" Rob lifted his chin in challenge.

"Anderson has a fine bunkhouse an' a good cook." Harker looked at Olga. He still didn't even know where they would live. He had married the young woman to keep from going to jail, but now he wanted her to be his wife. Her bright smile encouraged him and he continued. "Once Olga an' I get our place sorted out, you can stay with us if you aren't happy with Anderson."

"Why?" the boy's voice was soft, his eyes full of doubt. "I'm nobody. Why would you bother with me?"

Olga reached out, brushing her fingers across Rob's forearm. "Because we've all done foolish things before. Everyone deserves a second chance."

"What if I choose to go?" the boy's blue eyes flickered between the odd couple who had taken him in.

"Then you can go." Harker's words were soft. "But we'd much rather you came with us, so you can find a home in Needful." He looked down at Olga again and smiled. "I did, an' I wasn't even lookin' for it."

"Well, as long as you don't get any notions about me findin' a girl an' gettin' hitched. I'll come along with you for now, but when I feel like it, I'll light a shuck out without a backward glance."

In a matter of minutes, the trio had the horses saddled, gear packed and were ready to take the trail back to Needful.

"This isn't what I expected of this trip," Harker admitted, lifting Olga back into the saddle. His hands lingered on her waist as he looked into her warm eyes. "I thought I'd be leavin' Houston a free man, but you captured my heart along the way."

Rob swung into the saddle, turning his horse toward the road as he faced the rising sun. "If you two are gonna get all cow-eyed at each other, I'm not stickin' around."

Olga laughed and Harker released her, turning and swinging up on Scout. "Lead on then," he called. "There's only one Needful, Texas."

Four days of steady travel saw Olga home in Needful. She had never been so happy to see the dusty street lined with festive red, white, and blue.

Rob had seemed to relax a little with each day

on the road, and he spoke easily with Harker now, asking about wrangling and the town they would call home.

Harker reached across the gap between Scout and Bandit and took Olga's hand. "Looks like we're back where we started from. I'll drop you at the boardinghouse," he added. "Then I'm goin' to see if there's any place for rent in town." His gray eyes flickered over Olga, making her blush. "I'd like a little more time on my own with my new wife."

"What should I tell father," Olga asked, her voice pitched low.

"Nothing. Your Pa thought we were going on a honeymoon an' that's all he needs to know. Maybe one day we'll tell this tale, but for now…" Harker shrugged. "We get to know each other a bit better."

They pulled rein at the Hampton House and Harker swung down, pulling Olga from Bandit's back and stealing a quick kiss. "I'll be back soon." He turned to Rob. "The livery stable is around back. Will you take the horses there an' have Darwin put them up for a good feed. Then, when you're done, come inside, an' we'll have a good meal when I get back."

Rob nodded, rolling his eyes at Harker, who had his arm around Olga, but gathered the mounts and headed to the back of the boardinghouse.

"I don't think he's keen on the lovey-dovey stuff," Olga giggled.

"Well, he won't need to put up with it much longer."

"Do you think we can find a place to live?" Olga's butterflies were back, fluttering in her stomach as she thought of a future with Harker. She didn't know the man well, but she knew two things. She liked him a lot, and she knew he would never ask her to give up the dress shop.

"I don't know," Harker said, dropping his eyes. "I'll see what I can do, though. I know this isn't what you were plannin' on," he looked up again, "but," he looked sideways at her, "I'm comin' to care for you, an' I like who I am when I'm at your side."

Olga felt a rush of warmth cover her and her heart kicked up its beat. "That's the nicest thing anyone has ever said to me."

Harker shrugged. "Thank you for havin' me, Olga Fortuna."

"Thank you for figuring out what you wanted before it was too late for both of us," Olga grinned.

Harker pecked her on the cheek then nodded at the door. "I'm sure Heidi an' your pa will want to see you. So you'd best get inside. I'll be along for dinner."

Olga turned, planting a quick kiss on his lips then hustled into the Hampton House, skirts swishing on light feet.

"Olga. You're back!" Heidi rose from a table where she had been sitting folding napkins and hurried to her sister. "We didn't expect you so soon."

"I missed you," Olga said, grabbing her sister in a tight hug as she smirked at the lone figure still folding napkins at the table Heidi had left. "It looks like Mr. Boden is helping you today?"

Heidi's face went crimson, but she shook her head. "That man is always turning up and helping me with things," she whispered. "He seems to feel he owes me for helping him after Midas bit him."

"Uh-huh." Olga grinned at her painfully shy sister. "You look well. When's dinner?"

"Not for an hour," Heidi said. "Did you have a good trip to Houston? Was it everything you expected?"

"Nothing turned out as I expected," Olga laughed, smoothing her deep purple dress covered in white cross-hatching. "I even brought an extra body home with me."

Heidi's eyes went huge looking at her sister. "What?"

"We picked up a young man who needed a safe place to stay," Olga admitted. "He's settling the horses now and will be in shortly." Her smile brightened and she met her sister's eyes. "Harker is looking for a place to rent for us."

"Oh!" Heidi gasped. "Of course, you will want a place of your own now that you're married." She leaned in closer to her sister. "Is Harker a good husband?"

"Time will tell," Olga laughed then grew serious. "We discovered we like each other a great deal on this little journey. I know we're just starting out, but we both agreed to make a go of it." Her saucy smile returned and she winked at Heidi. "He doesn't want me to change a thing about myself or stop working in the dress shop either."

"That's wonderful." Heidi squeezed her sister again as the man called Boden cleared his throat. "I need to get back to work."

"Where's Father?" Olga asked. "Will I find him in his room?"

Heidi turned back to her sister halfway back to the work table. "Oh my no," she said, eyes wide again. "He's out driving Jude's mother about and showing her the spring flowers. The woman arrived in town the day after your wedding and has been busy ever since."

∞∞∞

Harker strolled along the main street of Needful, his eyes looking at every building in a new light. He'd never looked for anything like permanent lodgings before. Instead, his life had been a series of rest stops, bunkhouses and temporary housing.

A smile played along his lips. Olga was willing to take a chance on him, and he was determined not to let her down.

A flicker of movement across the street drew his eye and Harker watched Mr. Franco turn the sign on his door to 'Closed' as he stepped out the door.

"Evenin'," the old man drawled. Mr. Franco was an accomplished violin player and gave children music lessons in his little shop. In addition, he had subdivided his building offering Beth and Olga a section to use for their dress shop.

"Howdy," Harker offered back. "Nice day."

"It is," Mr. Franco looked up at the sky then toward the upper part of his building. "You one of Orville's crew?" the old man asked.

"No, sir." Harker tipped his head, studying the grizzled old man.

"Oh, well, I thought maybe he'd said when the men could get started on adding my room to the back of the shop."

"A room?" Harker asked. "I thought you lived upstairs." The cowboy's gray eyes rose, looking up to the top of the business.

"I do," Mr. Franco said, "but my knees are so bad now, I can't hardly climb the stairs. So I'm building out the back and will move in there as soon as it's ready."

"What you gonna do with the upper apartment?" Harker's eyes snapped back to the man. "Would you rent it?"

Mr. Franco turned dark eyes on the other man. "You interested?"

"I am." Harker's chest swelled. "I got married a couple of weeks ago and would like a place for my wife an' me to live."

"Oh," Mr. Franco grinned. "You married little Olga Fortuna. I remember now."

"Yes, sir." Harker grinned. "She runs the dress shop below you."

Mr. Franco rubbed his chin. "If you could get a crew together to move my things," the old man said, "You could move in this week. I can camp out in the shop until the new place is ready."

Harker's breath caught in his throat as a wave of joy swept over him. "Really? I can do that. I've got a few friends who wouldn't mind helpin' out. How's tomorrow sound?"

"Fine, fine," Mr. Franco chuckled. "You young folks sure are in a hurry. Of course, one day, you'll slow down."

"But not today," Harker hurried to the old man reaching out and shaking his hand. "Thank you. Wait until I tell Olga."

Practically skipping, the cowboy hurried back to the boardinghouse to bring the good news to his wife, a woman that he planned on spending the rest of his no longer lonely life with.

If he could organize a crew for the morning, they could be moved into their own apartment by that night. Pausing as he stepped up onto the boardwalk, Harker froze. "Hey," he called, pivoting on a boot heel. "How much?"

Mr. Franco chuckled, tucking a pocket watch into his pocket, before shouting a number across the street.

"That'll do!" Harker replied with a grin. "That'll do just fine."

His hand fell on the door handle, and he schooled his face to a serious scowl. It would be fun to surprise Olga after making her think he'd had no luck finding a place for them to live. "Imagine how thrilled she'll be to live right over the place where she works." The man chuckled, delighted with his good fortune. Things were coming up roses with sweet little Olga in his life.

∞∞∞

Olga looked up and smiled as Harker walked into the room. His eyes were downcast, his face grim.

"Oh, you didn't find anything," she said, hurrying to him. "It's all right. We can stay in the Hampton House for a while. Something will happen."

"I don't want you to be disappointed," Harker said. "You deserve a place of your own."

The way the cowboy talked thrilled Olga to her toes. He wanted her to have something to call her own, and it touched her heart. "We'll make do," she encouraged. "After all, how much room do we need? You'll be away chasing cows and I'll be busy in the shop."

"True, true," Harker mused as Olga led him to a table. "Still, we're just gettin' to know each other. It would be nice to have a place of our own where we could be alone."

Olga felt the heat rise up her neck at the way Harker said 'alone.' "You make it sound nice," she managed.

"It will be." Harker leaned in, his mouth close to her ear. "It can be just the two of us."

The door at the back of the room opened and Rob walked in. He was loaded down with bags and bundles and Harker laughed.

"Well, maybe not."

"Oh," Olga sighed. She had started to grow fond of the idea of spending time alone with Harker. He made her feel pretty in the oddest way.

Harker rose, heading for the boy, taking up some of Rob's burden. "Where do we take these?" he asked, his hands full.

Olga got to her feet and gestured for them to follow her. "We'll put my things in my room." She froze halfway up the stairs. "Uhm, Heidi and I share." Her eyes went wide, looking back down the stairs at Harker and Rob.

"Come along," a voice echoed from above. "I've made a room up for you."

Olga hurried to the top of the stairs where Ellen stood, her rose gold braid over one shoulder. "I saw you come in," the Hampton daughter-in-law smiled. "We'll put you up here tonight," she winked at Olga. "The boy can stay in the room down the hall."

Olga turned, meeting Harker's gaze, but his serious eyes told her nothing. When he shrugged, she turned back to Ellen, following her to one of the double rooms.

"One of the men can move the rest of your things from your old room," the woman said, her green eyes turning on Rob, who hung back at the top of the stairs. "I'll send one of the children with some fresh things for your friend as well," she whispered, leaning into Olga. "It's nice to have you home."

Olga opened the door, swinging it wide so Harker could enter and soon, he had placed their things on the bed.

"I'm startin' to like that word," Harker said, sitting on the edge of the bed and giving it a bounce. "Home. It has a nice ring to it."

Olga closed the door, following him to the bed and sitting down gingerly. After all the time they had spent alone together, she would have thought her nerves would be gone, but this was a new start. This moment was the beginning of a real relationship.

She could hear footsteps in the hall and Ellen's muted voice as she took Rob to his room and she let out a breath. "One day, we'll have a real home of our own," she said, dropping her hand onto Harker's. "A place to call our own."

Harker's lips twitched as he gazed down at her and Olga scowled. What did the man find so funny?

"We'll live above the dress shop," Harker spouted, the words tumbling from his twitching lips.

"What?" Olga gaped. "I thought…"

"You assumed I hadn't found us a place," Harker chuckled. "I never said that."

"You're terrible," Olga smacked the man across the chest with a light slap. He grabbed her hand, pulling it to him and lifting it to his lips.

"It was a surprise."

Olga looked up, meeting his gray eyes and laughed. "Yes, it is a surprise." Her heart fluttered. Not only was she surprised at the accommodations, she couldn't believe the way the handsome cowboy was looking at her.

"How did you manage that?" Olga's voice was breathy. "Mr. Franco lives there."

"He wants to live downstairs. So he's having Orville an' the Hampton boys cut the lumber and build an apartment at the back of the shop. If we move him tomorrow, he'll live in the shop until it's done."

Olga blinked astounded at the news. "We can move in tomorrow?"

"We sure can, darlin'," Harker laughed. "We'll have our own place an' the ride to work will be easy. At least for one of us."

Olga's heart soared and she turned, throwing her arms around the man and kissing him. She would hold nothing back from Harker Stevenson if he would have her. Today was the start of a brand new life. It would be a partnership where there were no secrets, no hesitation, and someday true love.

Harker's arms came around Olga and he kissed her back, filling her with a warmth and acceptance she had never known. He liked her. He liked her job. He even liked her clothes. What more could a girl want?

The kiss shifted as Harker pulled her back on the bed, making her realize there was much more to this marriage than she had fully understood. If he kept kissing her like this, they would both be late for supper.

Olga giggled as nimble fingers pulled loose the strings of her corset, any thought of dinner fleeing her mind like a wisp of a cloud. She had come to Needful as a bride and though it had happened in the strangest way, she was finally happy that her father had moved them all to the tiny town.

∞∞∞

"How'd I get roped into this again?" Beau Alder asked as he carried a chair down the stairs to the music shop below.

"You married into the mess," Jude Cane replied from the other side of the chair. "Apparently, these girls all think we work for them."

A sharp bark of laughter from Beau made everyone laugh. "They do keep us on our toes." His blue eyes flashed toward Adele and he smiled. "I'd say it's worth it, though."

"Boy, howdy," Harker agreed, waiting at the bottom of the stairs a trunk on his shoulder. "I didn't know a woman could have so much stuff."

"Olga has more dresses than the other three combined," Jude said. "I'm glad Fanny is more into books."

"Books are heavy," Harker snickered.

Jude lifted a shoulder as he pushed past Harker. "But they don't take up all the room in the cupboard."

The men chuckled as Adele walked over carrying a small bag. "Are you almost done?" she asked, her dark brows rising as the men laughed again. "Men," the oldest Fortuna daughter grumbled. "They make no sense at all."

Beau paused, offering her a grin. "But you love us anyway."

"We do," Adele agreed, brushing a kiss across his cheek as he moved by. "For some strange reason, we do."

Olga wiped her brow as a hot summer breeze blew through the open window. She had been married to Harker for two months now and together, they had settled into the little apartment, making a new life for themselves.

Each morning after breakfast, Harker rode out to the Bowlings' place for work while Olga made her way to the shop below to work with Beth. Smiling at the bright sunshine outside, Olga realized how happy she was. She had thought that getting married would mean losing the freedom she had so recently found, but the fact was she felt more content and more alive than ever before.

Moving to the window, the young woman poked her head through the opening, peering down the street. Perhaps she would catch a glimpse of Harker as he came home. So much had changed in the short time since they had returned to Needful.

The dress shop was getting busier as more special occasions were planned for the town. There had been a big party scheduled for the Fourth of July and there were real fireworks. The Fall Festival was in full planning mode now as well, and she and Beth volunteered to help sew decorations for the celebration.

A knock on the door below caught Olga's attention, and she looked down to see an older woman standing by the door.

"Hello Mrs. Cane," Olga called. "I'm afraid we're closed for the night."

"I just wanted a hem fixed." Mrs. Cane, Jude's mother, had arrived earlier that summer and was often seen in the company of Olga's father.

The woman seemed rather critical and controlling to her, but Olga didn't have to spend much time with her.

"Can't you come down and fix it?"

Olga's shoulders sagged. The heat of the day had been wearing on her, and she didn't want to open the stuffy shop and go back to work. Supper was on the stove, and she wanted nothing more than to sit and have a nice meal with her husband.

"Can't it wait until morning?" Olga tried.

"No. No, it can't. This is one of my best dresses and I want it done now." Mrs. Cane's mouth twisted in annoyance.

"I'll be right down." Olga moved to the stove, pushing the meal to the back of the iron surface. She would finish this job before Harker got back.

Tonight the young woman had even made a little extra dinner in case Rob came home to visit as well. The young man shadowed Harker in almost everything and was learning to be a good hand working cattle. Anderson Bowlings had given the boy a job and a place to live, now it was Harker's responsibility to teach him to be tops in handling horses and cows.

Olga trudged down the stairs feeling the heat intensify as she reached the shop. The windows and doors had all been shut up and the air was stuffy. Then, turning the lock, she opened the door letting Mrs. Cane in.

"Well, it's about time," the woman grumbled. "I thought you were going to leave me standing out there all day."

Olga bit her lip, holding back a sharp reply. She had put in a long day and her hands were already tired. "Let me see the dress," she said, holding onto her patience by a thread.

Mrs. Cane handed her a bag that the dress had been stuffed into. "I'd like it back tonight."

"Tonight?" Olga gaped at the woman. "My husband will be home soon and will want his supper."

"Surely, a clever girl like you doesn't allow a man to boss her around." The woman's blue eyes sparkled with a sharp light and Olga shook her head. She wanted to argue. She wanted to tell Mrs. Cane that Harker wasn't like that. They had agreed on how they would get on and so far, things had gone well.

Olga realized that somewhere between that first stolen kiss and now, she had grown very fond of Harker. The man made her laugh, kissed her senseless, and made her feel pretty. She smiled, thinking of him and wishing he were already home. There was so much more to the cowboy than others saw.

Harker Stevenson had a good heart. A heart he had all but buried long ago. Over the past few months, her relationship with the man had blossomed into a partnership and more.

Olga pricked her finger on the needle she was threading, jumping with a yelp. "Ouch," she said, shoving the finger into her mouth to keep any blood off the garment in her hands.

"That was clumsy." Mrs. Crane walked around the small room, looking at various fabrics. "I do hope you'll hurry," she continued. "I'd like to be back in time for dinner with Phineas at the Hampton House."

Olga bit back harsh words at the woman. She didn't know what her father saw in her, but perhaps he was lonely. All but one of his girls were married and in their own home. Surely it was a difficult adjustment for him.

Olga plopped down in her chair, not offering Mrs. Cane one and began sewing the hem of a rather dull dress back together. She wanted Harker to come home. She wanted to close the door and be alone with him and tell the man about her day.

Olga wondered how the cowboy's day had gone and lifted a simple prayer for his safe return home. Her time working with Beth had been helping her grow, not only as a wife but also as an individual soul with needs and a desire to love.

∞∞∞

Harker rode Scout to the livery stable, swinging down and tossing the reins to Darwin.

"Long day?" The other man grinned.

"Long month." Harker looked up at a relentless sun. "Wish we'd get some rain."

"You having to move cattle to the springs every day?"

"Just about," Harker said, taking a bandana from his pocket and wiping the sweat from his neck. "Thanks for lookin' after Scout an' my horses," he said, giving the livery keeper a wave. "It takes a load off of me."

Harker stalked across the street, his eyes troubled as he headed for the front door. He knew Olga would have supper ready and his stomach rumbled its desire for food. A hot cup of coffee, a good meal, and surely he would feel better.

It had been another long day of helping Rob figure out his place in the world as well as how to be the best cowhand he could be. The boy was working hard, but there was just so much to do. The boy was torn between being independent, able, to needy and it was wearing on Harker's mind.

A horse galloped by and Harker turned, seeing another cowboy ride by. Today Anderson Bowlings had been on the range again and offered Harker the job as foreman for the third time. The responsibility of the task weighed heavily on his shoulders. He was no one, a simple cowhand who had rambled from place to place for most of his life. He wasn't fit to manage a big ranch like that.

Maybe Bowlings had offered him the job thinking that now Harker was married, he'd want more responsibility. Harker shook his head, trying to push the thought away as he opened the door. He had enough to deal with already without being responsible for the Bolwings spread.

"Harker," Olga's sweet voice greeted him and the man squinted into the semi-darkness of the shop.

"I thought you'd be done for the day," Harker said, his voice coming out rough.

"Mrs. Cane needed a dress mended." Olga held up the dress as the other woman turned, looking at him with cool eyes.

"Mrs. Cane," Harker pulled his hat from his head, his gray eyes landing on the short, somewhat plump woman with dark hair and blue eyes.

"I hope you don't mind me borrowing your little wife," the woman simpered. "I just couldn't wait to have this fixed. I want to wear it for Sunday, you see."

Harker nodded, not seeing at all. It was only Thursday now. Surely the woman could have waited until Olga and Beth opened in the morning.

Olga's bright eyes flickered to him and she offered a slight smile. "I'll be up as quick as I can," she said. "I'll finish dinner when I come."

Harker nodded, his eyes darting between his wife and the older woman. Pushing his annoyance at not having Olga to himself away, he headed for the stairs with a wave of a dirt-encrusted hand. He would need to clean up before dinner anyway.

An hour later, Harker was still waiting for his dinner and his patience was growing thin. When Olga walked through their apartment door a few minutes later, he turned, not noticing the weary look in her eye.

"Why'd you open up for that woman?" Harker snapped. "I've been waitin' for over an hour for my supper."

Olga's mouth made a perfect O as she blinked at him. "Mrs. Cane was nitpicking," she stammered, surprised at Harker's annoyance. "I'll warm up our dinner now."

Harker paced the tiny kitchen while Olga hurried to the stove. His anger rising. Everyone seemed to expect something of him. Olga put him behind that snipe of a woman. Anderson was pressing him to take the foreman job and Rob stuck to his hip like a burdock when they were on the range.

Harker paced to the window, trying to catch a breath of fresh air, but the sweltering Texas heat had none to give.

"You'd think you could have some consideration to your husband," he growled. "Taking on a job after hours. You knew I'd be home. You knew I'd be tired an' hungry. I've been ridin' for hours with no break at all."

"I'm sorry," Olga said, turning, a puzzled look on her face. "You've never said anything before if work ran late."

"Well, maybe I should have." Harker was building a head of steam, all the pressure from work and life compressing it into a funnel that was sure to burst. "Isn't it enough that I work all day to provide a place for you? Don't you think I do enough that you could show some appreciation?"

A bright tear appeared on Olga's cheek but Harker ignored it, an overwhelming sense of being trapped prodding him onward like a set of spurs.

"I'm your husband. I should come first."

"You do come first." Olga snapped, turning and shaking the spoon in her hand at him. "I don't know who put a bur under your saddle but you have no call yelling at me. You agreed I could keep the shop and work. Are you changing your mind?"

"Maybe I am!" Harker shouted. "Maybe I want a wife that will sit home waitin' on me hand and foot. Someone who doesn't put herself ahead of me."

Olga gasped, and Harker could see the pain his words had caused, but he hardened his heart.

"Everyone wants something from me." He continued throwing his hands in the air. "You want me to let you work any time of the day or night. Rob wants me to make him into the kind of hand that earns top dollar an' Anderson wants to pass off his responsibility to me an' make me foreman of the ranch. Well, I won't do it. I don't need this. I don't need any of it." Harker threw up his hands. "This isn't who I am. I'm a rambler an' I'm done."

Grabbing for the door, the man yanked it open. "I'll send for my things later."

Olga flinched as the door closed shut on the man she had wed. The man she finally realized she loved. She had planned to tell him tonight just how special he was to her, how she loved him and was thankful for him. Now he was gone, and she was alone in an apartment that suddenly seemed cold.

Hot tears splashed down her face as she realized that Harker was gone. The pressure of life had been too much for him, and he had crumbled, turning to the way of life he knew best.

As the tears flowed, Olga began to understand what had happened. Harker felt pulled in too many directions at once. His sense of worthlessness, left to him by his mother's abandonment, had broken and sent him running.

"Lord," the young woman whispered, collapsing into a chair. "I love him. I know he's not perfect and that he has hurt I can't heal, but I don't want to lose him. Please, work in Harker's heart. Let him know that I love him and that even though he lost his temper, I don't hold it against him. Please," she sniffed again. "Bring him home."

∞∞∞

Harker had a saddle on Scout and was out the door before Darwin could say a word. Swinging up, the cowboy raced out of town on his weary horse, looking for an escape from all that pressed in on him. He felt like he couldn't breathe. Like someone had a stranglehold on his throat and was slowly squeezing the life out of him.

Two miles down the road, he slowed his heaving horse and hung his head. A vision of Olga's tear-stained face hit him between the eyes like a hammer, and he staggered, stepping down and collapsing into the dry grass of the prairie.

"Olga," he whispered, feeling a sharp pain in his chest. He'd ridden away. Left her behind and broken her heart.

Something hot and wet splashed on his pant leg, and Harker looked down at the spot where a tear had fallen. He wiped his eyes, surprised when his hand came away wet.

Was this how his mother had felt when she left? Had she been overwhelmed with the responsibility of a husband, son, and home? The cowboy shook his head. It didn't matter why she left, she had and left a ruin behind her.

"God," Harker looked toward the darkening sky. "I don't know what to do? I'm only a man. Weak, an' like the preacher said last Sunday made of dust. What am I to do? I'm not strong like some men. I don't have the will to take on all of this." He raised his hands, taking in the surrounding land. "What do I do?"

Flopping onto his back in the dust, Harker gazed into the sky where the sun sat low on the horizon. Darkness was coming but the rainbow hues of the sunset painted the end of the day in glorious light.

That's what Olga had done for him. She'd given him something to smile about. A stability and strength he didn't understand. She loved him, and though she had never said it, she had shown him in a myriad of different ways.

That stabbing pain in his heart returned, and Harker knew what he had to do. He loved that little girl. Not only had she given him a place to call home after so many years, but she had also given him her heart and her trust.

Pushing himself to his feet, Harker staggered to his horse and climbed on board. Scout pointed his nose back toward the barn he called home and together the pair made their way into Needful.

"Olga?" Harker pushed open the door of his home. The place was dark and smelled of cold food. "Olga?" Harker closed the door, moving into the place. "Honey, I'm sorry."

Something exploded from the hall, nearly bowling him over and Harker caught his wife in his arms. "You came back," she sobbed. "You came back."

Harker pulled her tight, his shoulders sagging with shame. "I'm sorry, honey," he soothed. "I was weak. I gave in to all the pressure an' ran."

Olga's chokehold on his neck made Harker smile sadly. He felt warm and welcome, not hobbled and trapped in her arms.

"Harker Stevenson, don't you ever do that to me again." Olga sniffed. "You nearly broke my heart. Don't you know I love you? Don't you know I don't care what job you take on? If you don't want to be a foreman, say no. If you want to ship Rob off to Dan Gaines and give him a new perspective, do that, but don't you ever leave me again."

"I won't, honey. I swear." Harker pulled her tighter. "I'm so sorry."

Olga slackened her grip on the man's neck, leaning back until she could look into his eyes. "And don't you yell at me for taking on a late customer either."

Harker felt a chuckle grow in his chest. His sassy wife was speaking her mind. "You knew me getting into this thing, and I haven't changed. So the next time you're feeling pressurized, you talk to me and we'll figure it out."

"Yes, dear." Harker felt his heart lighten. "Whatever you say, dear."

Olga's mild slap made him laugh and he dropped his head to hers, finding her mouth in the dark room. "I love you, honey," he said, pulling back to catch his breath. "I'm sorry I got overwhelmed."

"I understand," Olga said, running her hands over his cheeks. "Everything is so new, and we didn't plan this. But," her bright eyes danced in the dim light, "I love you and with that and a little faith, we can overcome anything."

"You think so?"

"I know it." Olga's smile flashed in the darkness. "Now, promise me you'll never pull anything like that again."

"I promise." Harker agreed.

"And promise me that you'll talk to me about things that are bothering you, or if people are asking more of you than you can give."

"I promise," Harker spoke again. "I'll never leave you, honey."

"Good." Olga took a deep breath that was broken with a sob that stabbed Harker in the heart. He never wanted to hurt her. He never wanted to let her down again.

"I don't know what I ever did to deserve you," he whispered into her neck.

A soft giggle brushed his cheek and he pulled back from the embrace, looking into Olga's lovely face. "What?"

"You got me drunk, so I had to marry you." Olga's laughter filled the apartment and Harker joined her, his heart finally free. Perhaps he would have bad days again. Maybe they would have their disagreements, troubles, and fears, but he knew that if he would confide in Olga, she would never let him down or leave him to figure it all out on his own.

"You're everything to me," Harker said. "I love you, Olga, an' I'll try to be the best husband I can be."

"You already are," Olga grinned. "You're the man I was meant for, even if I didn't know it at the start. God has a way of putting us where we belong and with the right person if we'll just let Him have His way."

Harker leaned in, kissing Olga's lips again. Today was another new start, and he would keep this woman at his side and in his heart until his dying day.

# *Epilogue*

"I don't see what Father sees in that woman," Heidi confided to Olga as they sat stitching table clothes for the Hampton House. "She's a harpy, plain and simple."

Olga looked toward the window where their father was helping Mrs. Cane down from a buggy. "Well, they're of an age, I suppose."

"Yes, but she isn't sweet like Miss Mercy was."

"No, but Miss Mercy loved Jacks and that's that."

"Do you think Pa will marry her?" Heidi asked, a tiny shiver running down her spine. "I bet she'd try to boss us if he did."

"Not me," Olga lifted her chin. "No one tells me what to do."

Heidi rolled her eyes. "Not even Harker?"

"I let him believe he's the boss," Olga giggled. "It's good for him."

"You love him, don't you?" Heidi grew serious.

"I really do." Olga's eyes danced with light. "He's more than I ever expected him to be."

"Do you think people can really change?" Heidi's voice was so low Olga had to strain to hear it.

"Yes. If they turn to God for help."

Heidi looked around the empty room as if searching for someone. "Boden Avery was a bounty hunter."

Olga's eyes went wide. "A killer?"

"Not that I know," Heidi admitted. "But he says he's done with that and doesn't want it to get in his way. The man says he wants to settle down in a little town like Needful and live a quiet life."

"With you?" Olga leaned in, trying to catch a hint of what her quiet, shy sister was thinking.

"No," Heidi dropped her eyes. "I don't want to marry and a man like that is dangerous."

"So you plan on working here for the rest of your life?" Olga looked around the Hampton House. "Pa won't like it."

"Pa doesn't get to decide." Heidi showed a rare spark of defiance for a moment then dropped her eyes to her work again. "Boden Avery needs a friend," the only single Fortuna girl continued. "I'm trying to be his friend, but I think he wants more."

Olga giggled. "Heidi, tell the truth, you like him."

Heidi shook her head, looking up and meeting Olga's eyes. "No," she said thoughtfully. "I feel sorry for him."

Harker walked into the dining room, a bright smile on his lips. "Beth told me you were here."

"What are you doing home so early," Olga stood to her feet, fear tugging at her heart.

"I took the job," Harker said. "I'm the new foreman at the Bowlings place." The man strode toward her, grabbing her around the waist and pulling her close. "What do you say to that?"

"You're sure?" Olga held her thoughts in reserve for a few moments, studying her husband's face.

"I'm sure."

"Whoopee!" Olga yelled, throwing herself into his arms. "I'm so proud of you."

"I couldn't have done it without you," Harker said, dropping a kiss to her lips. "I guess this is what love can do to a man."

### The End

### Sign up for my Newsletter and get a free book!

Subscribe  or follow on Bookbub at Facebook & AllAuthor

**More books in this series**

**Brides of Needful Texas**

Daliah

Prim

Peri

Beth

Ruth

Amanda

Adele

Fanny

Dear Reader,

Thank you for choosing to read my book. I hope you have enjoyed it as much as I've enjoyed writing it. If you enjoyed the story please feel free to leave a review wherever you purchased the book. Leaving a review will help me and prospective readers to know what you liked about this book. It is an opportunity for your voice to be heard and for you to tell others why the story is worth a read.

**About the Author**

Danni Roan, a native of western Pennsylvania, spent her childhood roaming the lush green mountains on horseback. She has always loved westerns and specifically western romance and is thrilled to be part of this exciting genre. She has lived and worked overseas with her husband and tries to incorporate the unique quality of the people she has met throughout the years into her books.

Danni currently lives in her thirty-six foot RV with her husband and is traveling the United States to see this beautiful country and experience its history first hand.

Danni and her 'every-day-hero' have one son who is attending college and finding his own way as his crazy parents experience the author life along with life on the road.

As a Christian Danni, believes strongly that God brings new challenges, and blessings into one's life to help them grow and she hopes that her words were both and encouragement and inspiration to you.

Made in the USA
Middletown, DE
14 April 2022